American Storytellers

Philip Baruth
American Zombie Beauty

Joyce Hinnefeld
The Beauty of Their Youth

Darrin Doyle
*The Big Baby Crime Spree
and Other Delusions*

The Big Baby Crime Spree
and Other Delusions

The Big Baby Crime Spree and Other Delusions

Stories

Darrin Doyle

Wolfson Press

The author is grateful to the editors of the publications where these stories first appeared:

"The Art of the Dead" appeared previously as "My Dead" in *H_NGM_N*; "The Odds" appeared in *Antietam Review*.

Cover design by Sky Santiago
Interior design by David James

ISBN: 9781950066063

Wolfson Press
Master of Liberal Studies Program
Indiana University South Bend
1700 Mishawaka Avenue
South Bend, Indiana, 46634-7111
WolfsonPress.com

Contents

Series Introduction and Preface ix

The Kaleidoscope   1
The Baby Doll 17
The Art of the Dead 39
The Odds 57
The Big Baby Crime Spree 69

Series Introduction and Preface

THE AMERICAN STORYTELLERS SERIES AT WOLFSON PRESS PRO-
motes genres of writing that have been neglected by major publishing houses. We join several other small presses in seeking to
provide a quality publishing outlet for books of shorter fiction
and nonfiction, such as the short story, the novella, the short
memoir, and the literary essay. Few commercial publishers today acknowledge a market for these forms. We believe, however, that much of the best American writing falls outside the
scope of the novel and the book-length work of nonfiction. A
flourishing mastery of the shorter genres is supported by a literary magazine culture and by longstanding practices in graduate
education. Most fiction writers, for example, begin their careers
as short story writers. For these writers a fine short fiction piece
is often not the first step in the development of a novel, but a
complete artistic statement. Shorter works, whether in essay or
story form, can coalesce into powerful collections that express
a sharp creative vision peculiar to the form. We hope to bring
rich collections of this kind to our ambitious readers by show-
casing the best short works by new and established writers.

Darrin Doyle is an artist of narrative condensation. Even
readers who know only his novels will have a sense of how

the succinctness of the short story form might allow him to accelerate his imagined social experiments into collisions that throw off as many sparks and quarks as a novel can. Doyle's stories, although sometimes full of dramatic incident, are essentially about the mind itself, exposed in the logic and pathos of various peculiar psyches. In the five stories collected here, you'll get to know characters whom you'd likely never meet in "real" life, or (if you're lucky) never know intimately, but who, once within your mind's orbit, begin to concern you and to challenge your humanity.

Doyle introduces us to grotesquely self-deceptive characters who are living on the edge (of legality, sanity, respectability). The power of these stories comes partly from Doyle's ability to amuse: the bleakest, most puzzling of fates can be funny if we can see ourselves distorted in the warped glass of the narrative. Each Doyle short story is like a disaster that you can't not keep staring at as it unfolds. The author takes us as close to the ugliness as we can bear, leaving only the degree of separation we need in order to be caught in the ethical borderland between sympathy and judgment. By enmeshing us in the quirky language of his characters' thoughts, he confronts us with alien mental worlds that are always unmistakably American.

In a story like "The Odds," we enter a mind stripped down to one or two obsessions and operating with the violent efficiency of a machine, sacrificing both the other and the self for personal triumphs that can never reach the emotional problem that needs to be solved. Although we may resist inhabiting the headspace of Doyle's main characters as they steam forward like freight trains with burnt-out brakes, they resemble us in their desire to beat the odds, even if they have less track than we do stretching ahead of them. They plot (like the muddled narrator of "The

Big Baby Crime Spree") a dramatic finale that they dream will repair their broken world.

Doyle writes like someone who has discovered a secret about humans, and he has. Like Nathaniel Hawthorne or Flannery O'Connor – both masters of the short story who were also subtle students of social psychology – Doyle writes stories that spring from a central insight into human nature, a vision of inner conflict as a microcosm of social and historical tensions. Hawthorne formulates his theory at the end of his story "Wakefield," about a man who absconds from his own life, wife, and friends, to relocate (for "upwards of twenty years") a short distance from his urban home: "Amid the seeming confusion of our mysterious world, individuals are so nicely adjusted to a system, and systems to one another, and to a whole, that, by stepping aside for a moment, a man exposes himself to a fearful risk of losing his place forever." Hawthorne's social vision was one in which communities, through relations extending almost infinitely, define the meaning of people's lives for all practical purposes. Rejecting Ralph Waldo Emerson's ideal of self-reliance, Hawthorne shows people to be helplessly dependent on others for meaning, even as they (sometimes tragically) view themselves as free, able to say yes or no to the world.

Doyle locates a similar conflict in the current extreme fantasy of individual ambition (becoming famous, striking it rich). This dream ironically turns life into a distraction from living. (In one of his novels, he envisions this impossible, destructive success in a remarkable girl who eats the city of Kalamazoo, rebelling against ordinary life by consuming its infrastructure. In the process she becomes both incredibly famous and thoroughly alienated from ordinary social satisfactions.) In Doyle's vision, the demons of fraud, cowardice, and wishfulness lurk in the depths of the American psyche. Flattered by the "American Dream," we lie to ourselves. Toiling under an absurd pressure to appear to be winners, we are essentially dishonest. His previous story collection, *Scoundrels Among Us*, exposes the failing lives of the ne'er-do-wells we know too well. "Scoundrel" is a harsh designation, but it contains more than a hint of the merely rascally, or small-time, encompassing the swindler and the rogue, the charlatan and the son of a bitch. As we see in the defeated characters of the Southern Gothic tradition, there is a shabby grandeur to these Midwestern strivers who are careening toward a brick wall at full throttle.

The disastrous outcome is, for Doyle, the starting point for honestly assessing who we are. You won't easily find yourself in this new collection, certainly not altogether willingly, but these seductively grotesque and (especially in the case of the title piece) slyly hilarious stories reveal how our private delusions divide us from one another while making it almost impossible for us to understand ourselves. It's as if there were a scoundrel within each of us, a demon that lingers like an unwelcome houseguest until it owns us. So we continue, secretly striving to keep the big dream alive, holding out for the miracle that must surely restore us one day.

Joseph Chaney, Series Editor
American Storytellers

For Courtney

The Kaleidoscope

ON THE EVENING JERRY AND KATHY MOVED INTO THEIR NEW apartment, Ray Peterson stopped over. He weaved through the maze of boxes in the dining room, shook Jerry's hand, and gave Jerry a quarter-ounce of weed. "A welcome-home present," Ray said.

Jerry thanked him. Ray resembled the same Ray who had commandeered the grill at the *Safe Travels, Jerry and Kathy!* barbecue eighteen months earlier (he still bore the trademark mutton chops and head of brown Einstein hair), but his torso had thickened and his face was unnaturally bloated and red. Jerry told Ray that it was nice to see him, and they retired to the couch to smoke a couple of bowls.

Ray was an acquaintance of Jerry's who owned some rental houses. Ray had a wife named Veronica and two preschool-aged daughters. He had explained to Jerry over the phone that they were happy to rent the Park Place unit at a lower rate than they'd been asking because the refinishing of the hardwood floors had left a coat of red dust on the window ledges, shelves, and doorknobs that they hadn't gotten around to cleaning. Jerry had said they didn't mind the inconvenience; they needed a place right away.

After smoking, Jerry and Ray stared at the quiet audience of boxes, end tables, and furniture. For Jerry, the wordlessness felt comfortable. His wife Kathy could be heard upstairs, unpacking and dusting surfaces. Jerry liked the sensation of being away from her, separated by an actual floor, after so many consecutive months of being joined at the hip while living abroad.

Jerry offered Ray some of the cold pizza on the coffee table. Ray chewed a slice and plucked thoughtfully at his left sideburn, which was shaped like a backward L.

"I have a tumor in my gut," Ray said.

Jerry said he was sorry. He tried to summon another word or phrase that might be helpful. Nothing came. He considered asking if the tumor was malignant but then couldn't remember the opposite of malignant – the good (or at least not-so-bad) tumor – so he gave up and issued a grunt meant to express indignation.

"It's in my adrenal gland," Ray continued, in the clinical tone of someone describing the broken headstock of a guitar. "That's why I've been having these weird symptoms. The weight gain. This tomato head." He gestured toward his face, which to Jerry's surprise wore a broad, if manic, smile. "Sometimes I open my eyes at night and see people in our bedroom. I'm in REM sleep but feel completely awake. The people talk to me and everything. I cracked a rib a year ago just from laughing too hard." He expulsed a giggle as if to test whether another rib would break.

"Can they operate?"

"They tell me surgery will get rid of it," Ray said. "I'm going in in a couple of months."

✦

While it was upsetting that his vocabulary had shrunk in that moment (benign, goddamn it), Jerry consoled himself that news of Ray's sort was not normal to hear from anyone, let alone a guy he'd known for ten years but had never talked with about anything more substantial than Funkadelic albums and fog machines. Jerry had played bass in Fonzarelli's Thumb while Ray was the lead guitarist in The Impossible Crutches. The two bands had formed a friendship, booked shows together, covered each other's songs, shared dreams of success. Now, four years after the groups disbanded, Jerry saw Ray as the last remnant remaining from that time period – a nice remnant, to be sure, but a remnant nonetheless.

Kathy was saddened by the news. She was concerned about Ray and his family. He was so young. Only thirty-two. She wondered aloud what would happen to Veronica and the girls if Ray died.

Kathy's hair was arranged carefully on the pillow beneath her head. She watched Jerry undress; it was apparent by her silence that she was visualizing Jerry with a tumor, though her silence couldn't tell Jerry on which part of his body she'd placed it.

They had moved to Japan to teach English. They lived for one year in the mid-sized city of Nara, then traveled for six months through Cambodia, Thailand, and Malaysia on twenty dollars a day. Now, at last, they were back in Michigan. They'd returned to Kalamazoo thinking of it as their home. They were ready to get settled, stop living out of six-dollar hotel rooms, stop carrying their lives in backpacks. They were ready to find careers, maybe even buy a house or have a child.

One week after moving into Park Place, the Portage Public Library rehired Kathy in her old position in the Youth Department. The salary was exactly what Jerry and Kathy needed. They popped the cork on a bottle of Korbel Brut. How had she managed to step into the same job that she'd quit eighteen months before? Jerry and Kathy asked each other this rhetorical question as they got drunk, while he washed dishes and she sliced cheese for a midnight snack. It was good fortune, they said. Good timing. Good, good, good.

Jerry had received a master's degree in Practical Writing just before they left America, and as he drained his fourth glass of bubbly he announced to Kathy his plan to look for any work that didn't involve the three F's: food, factories, and fucking retail. No pizza restaurants, no magazine stands. No clothing stores or copy shops. No door-to-door solicitation, no telemarketing. No caulking glue factories or temp agencies. Nothing minimum wage, nothing with walk-in customers. He'd had enough. He wanted to drive a limo. Or be a private detective. Or model nude at the Art Institute.

Kathy didn't seem to mind Jerry's pickiness. She never actually used the word "pickiness" – she called it "selectivity" – but Jerry figured he knew what she meant. She insisted that he take his time. Her salary was enough to live on. She wanted him to be happy. She wanted him to find a job like hers, something he could truly enjoy. While he job-hunted, she added, he could finish unpacking boxes and dusting ledges – whenever he got the chance. It was always nice, she insisted while the sink drained with a wet sucking sound, to have one person at home who didn't work.

✳

On Kathy's 9:00 AM days, Jerry slept until long after she left. On the days she worked at 1:00 PM he stood at the back door and kissed her goodbye before walking to the Laundromat to buy a newspaper so he could keep an eye on the Want Ads, which he read while reclining in the easy chair in front of the picture window that overlooked the park.

Their duplex occupied a two-story house that had been built in the 1930s. In the adjacent apartment lived another young married couple who drove a Toyota Corolla the color of an open wound and a Ford Taurus the color of a Band-Aid. "The perfect Yin and Yang," Jerry called them. They made no noise whatsoever, except with their plumbing.

There was no street in front of the duplex. Instead, there was a park crisscrossed by an 'X' of sidewalks. Another sidewalk encircled the park perimeter. Wrought-iron lamps stood at planned intervals, lighting the paths, and towering oaks extended their snow-bearing arms over the scene. In the wintertime the park was sparsely-trafficked and quiet, like an elderly librarian whose mere presence said, *Shhhhh*. The tree shadows looked like spilled wine on a white tablecloth.

One afternoon, Jerry went out on the porch to get the mail. He noticed a pair of embedded brown turds in the snow directly in front of their apartment. He saw paw prints and squirts of yellow piss. Jerry seemed to remember a law prohibiting dogs from doing their business in people's yards, but was it truly a law, or just a gentlemen's agreement? And even if it was a law, whom would he call? The police? He decided that it didn't matter since nobody came to visit anyway. The mail in the box was all junk.

Within a month, the *Kalamazoo Gazette* hired Jerry as a freelance writer. Margaret the editor handed him a stack of work – play and concert previews, profiles of local painters, sculptors, composers, and rock bands. His two-month supply added up to nine assignments. Each assignment paid fifty dollars. The money was a pittance, but the position meant Jerry could give up the uncomfortable process of searching through the newspaper with Sharpie in hand, circling and skimming (more skimming than circling), pondering which tree he would prefer chaining himself to for the next five, ten, twenty years.

Kathy greeted the *Gazette* news with a polite smile. With television light flickering in her eyeballs, she mumbled, "Great."

She was tired; she had worked ten hours that day. What looked like pity in her brief glance, Jerry decided, must be exhaustion.

She rested her head on Jerry's shoulder and soon fell asleep. Later, he lifted and carried her up the stairs. He put her into bed.

*

Jerry conducted interviews over the telephone. He recorded the interviews with the answering machine. Then he played the answering machine and used a hand-held recorder to record the conversations. Then he went upstairs to his desk and used the hand-held recorder to transcribe the interview onto the computer.

It only took two hours to write each article once he had the facts in front of him.

Jerry had lots of free time. He couldn't figure out what to do with it. Night after night, he flipped through TV channels (all in English, which continued to surprise him); he listened to the college radio station; he surfed the Internet for pornography and funny videos. Morning's first chirping of birds sent him stumbling into bed, where he lay awake thinking about the tumor in Ray's gut and wondering if he should give Ray a call. Jerry had driven the last two rent checks (December and January) to Ray's house but had simply dropped the envelope into the mailbox without ringing the doorbell, hustling back to the car in a pretend rush to get somewhere.

In the light of day, however, the process of dialing the Petersons' number and actually talking to Ray about the tumor (or *not talking* to him about the tumor) seemed complicated and unnecessary. Besides, Jerry reasoned, an ill person like Ray would be napping during the afternoons. And if he weren't napping, he would certainly want to be alone with his family. Rather than call Ray, Jerry usually looked out the picture window at the constellation of feces on the tiny lawn.

*

Jerry ate 2:00 PM breakfasts of tomato soup and crackers at the dining room table. Sometimes the girl next door climbed the exterior wooden staircase to her attic apartment, and he watched her. He performed household chores like washing dishes, bagging trash, tossing dirty clothes into the laundry. He continued the battle of Paper Towel vs. Red Dust, because Kathy discovered, daily, new surfaces he had "neglected," and she taped scribbled notes to this effect on the refrigerator, kitchen counter, stereo, and TV screen (each day a different spot and a different note with nearly the same wording).

Without fail, by the time Kathy arrived home from work, Jerry's powerful, all-day urge to confront her about her badgering had shriveled into a nagging whisper that he readily ignored; for Kathy's part, she appeared too tired to discuss much of anything.

Even when she gripped the knob of the linen closet cupboard and came down with red fingers she said nothing, but she made a grand display of marching to the sink with her hand held forth like a flag. They avoided each other until she fell asleep on the couch and he helped her up the stairs into bed.

*

Jerry spent twenty minutes a day staring at the park through the picture window, sipping his coffee. He and Kathy had talked about it; they both were feeling profound culture shock from America.

In Japan, the language had been a mystery. The sounds that came from people's mouths had no meaning. On his daily train ride into Osaka for work, he'd felt protected: there was never the worry of having to talk to anyone, no bristling at inane overheard conversations. He could bury his face in a book, glancing up now and then to marvel at the fast-asleep *salaryman* who stood with one hand gripping the plastic overhead handle as if showing the world that despite appearances some part of him always remained awake. Jerry and Kathy shopped the *shotengai* in a state of happy oblivion, pointing with amazement rather than cynicism at the wax tempura in the display windows, at the ten-inch platform shoes on tanned Japanese girls with bleached hair, at the arcade crane game with a live lobster prize. They'd been like visitors on a faraway planet, viewing innocently distorted replications of the world they'd left behind.

When they returned to the United States, a collection of mysteries vanished from their lives. Americans were noisy, curt, aggressive, and worst of all, recognizable. Grown adults, in broad daylight, conducted business wearing sweatpants. Overweight schoolchildren picked their noses at bus stops. Domesticated animals defaced lawns at will. Pickup trucks the size of small buildings blotted out the sky. Even billboards were confrontational:

Which part of 'Thou Shalt Not' didn't you understand?
– God

But looking out over the park, with its snow-draped benches and solemn iron lamps, Jerry decided that he should feel happy. They were now secure. They could speak the language; they could learn from the local news; if they got sick, the doctor would understand their ailments. Streets were familiar. Family lived within one hundred miles. Taco shells and canker sore medication could be found in every corner grocery. In this heated apartment with an American kitchen, Kathy could (and would, once she found the time) cook to her heart's delight.

One afternoon, Jerry stood at the picture window and watched a young man with a goatee stroll down the sidewalk at the pace of an altar-bound bride. A fluffy, unleashed white dog trotted alongside the man, poking its jittery nose here and there into the snow. The dog certainly weighed less than Jerry's dictionary.

The dog stopped in front of Jerry and Kathy's duplex. It squatted and dropped four brown nuggets out of its behind. The owner also stopped, his hands buried in his jacket pockets. His face was expressionless; clouds of frozen air issued from his mouth. The dog scratched at the snow, squirted urine, and scampered away. The owner resumed his solemn, disinterested walk. At the window, Jerry waved his arms to get the guy's attention, without success.

Over the next week, Jerry witnessed this again and again. It wasn't only the fluffy white dog. There was a full-grown husky that roamed the park, unsupervised by the hippies three houses down. The husky enjoyed relieving himself, both liquidly and solidly, on Jerry and Kathy's lawn. Other dogs followed suit. Tubular land mines and yellow sunbursts decorated the snow.

"I don't get it," Jerry said to Kathy, while they lay in bed. "There's a whole park out there, and these people let their dogs take a dump in our yard. It's not even a yard. It's ten feet of grass."

Kathy agreed. She listened to his complaints. She had listened to his complaints while they sat in front of the TV. She had listened to his complaints as she brushed her teeth. She had listened to his complaints after sex. She had agreed with him. She still agreed. It was a problem. Those people were assholes. "You ought to tell them to stop," she said. She closed her eyes as if to fall asleep. She wanted him out of the room but probably didn't think saying so would have any effect.

Jerry read for a while before turning off the light. He climbed out of bed, went downstairs, and drank four beers on the porch, where his nose burned from the cold.

Ray Peterson went into surgery to remove the tumor on his adrenal gland. He made it through the operation and e-mailed a photograph of the tumor to his friends. It looked like a decayed potato, with all sorts of unruly tentacles sticking out here and there. A ruler beside the tumor showed that it was two inches long.

Jerry was pleased to see the tumor, pleased that it had been cut from Ray's body before it could do any damage. It inspired Jerry to write a return e-mail. He clicked away on the keyboard, the words spilling out effortlessly. A tumor, he wrote, was just a physical manifestation of tension and dissonance, a waste product that the body needed to expulse. Thus, even though it was terrible what Ray had gone through, a strong person like him who was a fantastic guitar player with a great sense of humor and two beautiful daughters and a lovely, intelligent wife would certainly emerge from this ordeal as an even better human being. Jerry sprinkled his missive with shared memories of Fonzarelli's Thumb and The Impossible Crutches. As a finale, he used his Japanese dictionary to assemble a quote that he was pretty sure translated roughly as "Sorrow is the shortest leash," by which he was trying to say that distance made everything better.

Jerry proofed his e-mail before sending it. As he read, he recalled how just a few months ago he hadn't even been able to think of the word "benign," let alone any words of consolation for Ray. He pictured himself at that moment – sunken into the sofa, stoned and slack-jawed, twiddling his thumbs beside this guy who had cancer eating his gut.

Jerry realized shamefully that he hadn't even once attempted to follow up about Ray's condition. Ray would see this e-mail as a half-assed, far-too-late apology. Or worse, he would think Jerry had been scared of the tumor, afraid to come near the disease. Jerry was obviously sending this belated e-mail as a surrogate for his actual presence.

Also, he and Ray had never been *that* close; even in the band days, they hadn't hung out more than five or six times a year. Wouldn't this gushing letter sound phony?

Jerry deleted the e-mail and typed that he was glad Ray made it through okay and if there was anything he could do, to let him know. A few minutes later, Ray responded: "Just send your positive thoughts my way."

The *Gazette* job was getting old fast. In fewer than two months, the parade of strangers droning on about their projects made Jerry impatient and tired. He attempted to write transcendently within his 750-word limit. He loathed the typical butt-kissing community articles but ultimately found this mode impossible to avoid. The editors hacked out any crumb of creativity or constructive criticism. The "reviews" were merely thinly disguised promos; the community didn't want to hear that its fine arts were, in actuality, crappy arts. Whether dealing with overwrought plays *(Playwright Franklin added, "The character tries hard to protect whatever small part of himself he has in his suitcase, the symbol of his secret or lack of secret, his dream or lack of dream")*, gospel groups in need of hyperbole *(Drummer Javon Choen was a standout, his counter-rhythms and dynamic swells helping lift the music not just to the ceiling, but through it)*, or deluded rock bands *(When asked if their songs are serious or not-so-serious, Gorley said, "A little of both. If you come to one of our shows, you'll leave with a whole basketful of emotions")*, Jerry could only give praise. At the end of the day, he was nothing but a pitchman.

Nights, while Kathy slept, Jerry stood outside, his face cut by the frigid wind, shoveling frozen dog poop from his yard and tossing it onto the sidewalk. The following mornings (1:00 PM) with coffee mug in hand, he hid in the corner of the picture window to observe the dog owners. They inevitably spotted the mounds of feces just before sidestepping, pointing, and warning their friends.

Jerry's message wasn't getting through: the dogs continued to drop loads while the owners yawned. Was this the way things were done in America? Had there been a secret meeting while he and Kathy were away? Jerry seemed to be misunderstanding the rules. And Kathy didn't appear to care either that their yard – what little yard it was – was being systematically violated.

Jerry considered painting a sign and stabbing it into the dirt, but what would it say? *NO POOP, PLEASE?* He would look ridiculous. He considered calling the city commissioner and filing a complaint, but which department? It would entail endless red tape, as aggravating as the poop itself. Or how about a reasoned, rational talk with the dog owners – a sort of sit-down, where they negotiated poop boundaries while Jerry served hot cocoa and windmill cookies?

What a silly, stupid problem when the world was filled with cancerous tumors.

He longed to tear open the door and scream profanities. Instead, he stomped through the apartment holding conversations in his head, talking out loud to the phantom dog-owners, working himself into a private frenzy.

◆

On the first of March, Jerry drove to the Petersons'. He rang the doorbell. Ray's wife answered, flanked by her daughters. Veronica Peterson was a short, pale woman with an awkwardly pretty face, crooked teeth, and muddy bangs cut evenly over her eyebrows. Jerry handed her a white envelope that contained the rent check. He smiled at the Peterson girls, who clung to their mother's pant legs. They stared up at Jerry with thumbs in their mouths. Veronica invited him inside. Her eyes were puffy and red. She'd been crying, but Jerry didn't ask the reason.

He went to the basement. Ray was in the workroom wearing safety glasses. He greeted Jerry with a wave and asked him to shut the door.

Ray produced a joint from a tinderbox. They smoked it. Ray asked Jerry if he needed any weed. Jerry said he could always use some, so Ray gave him a quarter-ounce in a tightly rolled baggy. Jerry said he didn't have any money on hand, but that he could definitely go to a bank machine. Ray told him it was free.

"This guy I know grows it," he said. "He gives it to people who smoke, and we give it to other people who smoke." He said it was a nonprofit, positive karma sort of thing, to keep the creativity flowing and whatnot. Before Jerry had a chance to say thanks, Ray put a wooden kaleidoscope into his hand.

It was eight inches long and feather-light. The wood was un-polished and rough, a pale cream color. It felt delicate but sturdy. Jerry looked into the kaleidoscope. He pointed it toward the fluorescent light over the workbench. He rotated the kaleidoscope and watched flowers of color bloom, shrink, and bloom again.

"It's for the kids," Ray said.

"Impressive," Jerry said.

Jerry held the kaleidoscope, looked at it, turned it over in his hands. He could hear the shards of glass rolling around inside. The noise was soft, not unpleasant, not like something shattered beyond repair.

"You look good," Jerry said. Some of the bloating had left Ray's face, and the redness in his cheeks and neck was less pro-nounced.

"Thanks. I'm in pain all the time, though. They pumped me full of air to make room to operate. All that air's still inside me."

He ran his fingers over his belly. "Hurts like hell."

"It must be better than before."

"I guess," Ray said. He examined the joint between his fingers. "I just found out I have another tumor. In my brain. It's always something." He started laughing. Behind the safety glasses, his eyes became slits. His laughter attained a pitch and consistency that made it sound like someone was tickling him.

"Are you serious?" Jerry said, and he knew that he might as well have said nothing. Eye contact was uncomfortable. Jerry looked at the cement floor, at his boots.

"They can't operate for a while. Not until I get healthy again." He continued scrutinizing the roach. "I guess it's not doing any harm. They say it's not hurting me. Crazy to think about that thing just sitting up there. I'm gonna kill this." He squashed out the roach and put it in an Altoids tin.

Jerry said he had to get going. He told Ray to let him know if he needed anything. He thanked Ray for the weed and returned the kaleidoscope to its place on the workbench.

★

The fluffy white dog made a visit that afternoon. Jerry stood at the picture window. The telephone rang. Jerry let the answering machine get it. The goateed dog owner stood at his usual distance ten paces up the sidewalk, blameless, one hand pressing a cigarette to his lips, the other hidden in his jacket pocket. The voice on the machine was Margaret from the *Gazette*. She said there were more pieces for Jerry to write, and she rattled them off, and she said to please give her a call because she was going to Milwaukee next week for a wedding, and someone needed to take these things.

Jerry knocked on the picture window – *clunk clunk clunk*. It sounded like a giant fish tank. He knocked again, and the glass shook.

The dog owner looked up at Jerry. Jerry pointed at the fluffy white dog, which was squatting, depositing its shit. Its teeth were exposed in something like a grin, something like a child at a circus.

Jerry jabbed the window with his finger until he thought the glass might shatter, then he slapped the window with the palm of his hand. The dog owner removed the cigarette from his mouth, blew his smoke. He called to his dog once, twice, three times. The dog didn't understand, or didn't care, or wasn't paying attention.

The Baby Doll

IT WAS THIRTY MINUTES BEFORE SUNRISE, A CHILL ON THE BREEZE, the world undefined. Streetlamps threw hazy light. At the curb in front of the house, Gary embraced Meredith and kissed the baby. He went to the rear of the Civic and loaded suitcase, duffel bag, stroller, and portable crib into the trunk while Meredith strapped Barrett into the car seat.

Gary leaned in the driver's window before Meredith was to pull away. As their lips touched, he heard the rumble of an approaching engine. A wood-paneled station wagon slowed behind him; an arm emerged from its window and tossed a newspaper. The lopsided car roared to the next block.

"That asshole drives too fast," Gary said.

Meredith told Gary to behave.

"Call me when you get there," Gary answered.

He stood waving on the sidewalk as she and the baby disappeared around the corner.

The paperman had missed by a mile. Gary left the bone of news in the center of the lawn, well out of reach of the neighboring Bed & Breakfast's sprinkler, which already, at this early hour, waved its towering hand. When he reached the porch, Gary made sure to wipe his slippers on the welcome mat. He thought of a cat, hurling litter.

★

Gary worked at Boogie Records. The store stocked CDs, DVDs, and vinyl. Gary liked to impress customers with his knowledge. He knew which label had issued the first Black Flag 7", who populated the gang chorus on Agent Orange's 1981 *Living in Darkness* LP, and which Cure import had been pressed on glow-in-the-dark picture disc. Boogie provided a steady income while Gary composed and shopped his jingles to local companies.

The soundtrack of Gary's childhood was comprised of Dr. Pepper (*I'm a Pepper, he's a Pepper, you're a Pepper, she's a Pepper/Wouldn't you like to be a Pepper, too?*), Burger King (*He's the marvelous, magical Burger King/He can do most anything/He can make magic, and burgers, and fries/And here's something new right before your eyes!*), and other commercial tunes. Gary often argued that there hadn't been a significant original jingle since Doublemint's "Double Your Refreshment." In their golden era (the '70s and '80s), these 30-second opuses invoked dreams, tapped into possibilities: *Kiss a little longer, hug a little longer. Reach out and touch someone. Get a little closer, don't be shy.*

The key was to tie the product to a belief or desire; Gary strove for this connection in the lyrics he scribbled in his notebook. He had played guitar and co-written songs in a punk band for a few years. Catchy melodies came easily to him, but he labored at the words.

If Gary could sell just one of his jingles, he would not only be validated in Meredith's eyes, he would be more likely to sell another. Artistic success, he believed, was like bowling: hit that first pin, and others would topple. In two years, he had been rejected twenty-seven times by local companies, but this was part of the game. He was a community college dropout with no intention of returning to school. He was in it for the long haul, and one day, he would sells his jingles if it killed him.

Meredith had quit teaching to stay home with the baby, a move Gary supported even though they were beginning to feel the pinch. They paid mortgage on time, but they disconnected the cable TV. Gary took the bus to work. They never ate out. They were on Medicaid. Meredith clipped coupons and gave up her yoga class. Half of their wedding dinnerware was chipped. The baby hadn't cost too much – not yet – but soon there would be sneakers, winter clothes, piano lessons, bicycles, college.

Meredith handled the finances, and she was beginning to worry. Using whistles and sighs, she disparaged the size of Gary's checks and – it seemed to Gary, though she never said it outright – the record store itself. She referred to it as "the toy store." As in, "What time do you work at the toy store tomorrow?" This may have been due to her general apathy toward music: other than a pair of K-Tel compilations that served as childhood mementoes, she owned none of the one thousand albums that dominated their living-room shelves. Gary believed that his wife equated music, especially rock music, with immaturity, and her support for his passion was waning. Meredith insisted that her "toy store" remark referred to Gary's young coworkers. He didn't dispute this assertion.

On the issue of income, he defended himself. Both Gary and Meredith came from middle-class homes. As a child, Gary had experienced rough times, financially and emotionally, after his father's death. His mother had raised him on a grocery clerk's salary, and it was during these years that he had cemented his priorities. He reminded Meredith that he had entered into this marriage believing neither of them preferred paychecks over inner peace. Financial worry caused 90% of divorces, he said, so couldn't they remove it from the equation? In fact, a Spartan existence would be liberating. He offered a Thoreau line he had recently seen on the internet: "Men have become the tools of their tools."

Gary would never let Barrett go hungry. He would auction his vinyl on eBay before that boy missed a meal. They had a roof over their heads, clothes on their backs. Most important, they had Barrett. If the baby didn't satisfy her, Gary asked, what would? What else did she need?

★

Nine hours after his family left town, Gary was strolling along the sidewalk, returning from the record store. Low gray clouds were ushered by an insistent wind, like ghosts evacuating a natural disaster.

As he passed the B&B, Gary nodded at Miss West, the proprietor, whom he had never met. She was an elderly widow and was totally blind. According to Meredith, Miss West had made an unusual request during her Welcome to the Neighborhood visit one year ago. After presenting Meredith a basket of cheese, Miss West had insisted they (Meredith and Gary) should nod in greeting rather than call out "Hello" if they ever saw her sitting on her porch. Her goal, apparently, was to "challenge her hearing."

If hearing was the sense Miss West relied on to detect passing pedestrians, then hers rivaled a bat's.

But Gary questioned whether Miss West had actually given this instruction. He even questioned her blindness. Meredith – elementary school teacher and former salutatorian – made a hobby of inventing stories solely to see if Gary would believe them. To Meredith, this wasn't lying; this was *practical joking*. Sometimes it was small things. She told Gary that his mom had called; she giggled when he called her back. She told Gary his favorite TV program had been moved to Thursday nights. She switched the salt and sugar. She taped the kitchen sprayer so it soaked his chest when he turned the faucet.

Other times, the jokes were more elaborate. She set the clocks an hour ahead so he arrived to work early. She convinced Gary that his sneaker brand had been recalled because the dye might wash off in the rain, soak through his socks, penetrate his skin, and kill him. He'd gone so far as to box up and UPS his shoes to Converse, expecting a check for a new pair, before Meredith let him in on the "joke." He had laughed – he always laughed – and said that her jokes were, in fact, to him, "*im*practical."

Now Miss West nodded in Gary's direction without raising her hand. Her attitude was impossible to glean: the stucco porch wall concealed the lower half of her face, and her sunglasses resembled gray coins over her eyes. Was she laughing? Scowling? Had she really nodded in return?

Gary mounted his slope of lawn and retrieved the rubber-banded *Enquirer*. It felt like a soggy brick. He saw that the B&B sprinkler, now off, had been repositioned. The paper was soaked.

Inside the house, two messages blinked on the answering machine. Gary listened while plunking the newspaper into the can below the kitchen sink: "Wanted to let you know we made it okay. And *somebody* only took one tiny nap the whole trip. He's a grump. All right. Bye."

Gary was happy they'd made it to Michigan. It was his first time away from his four-month-old son. Days earlier, Gary had imagined Meredith and Barrett as corpses on a mortician's table. For five minutes, he'd sat on the toilet, chin between his knees, unable to take his eyes off the cupboard below the sink (behind which Charmin, scale, and First-Aid kit sat in darkness). He felt sick not only because of the vision, but because he worried that some part of him actually wanted them to die.

The next voice on the machine was a man named Daniel Bruce from Spad's Pizza, whose long job title included the word "marketing." He wanted to discuss Gary's jingle. It had "a good deal of potential." Daniel Bruce left his phone number.

It was after 5:00 PM – too late to return Mr. Bruce's call – so Gary microwaved the leftover hot-and-sour soup Meredith had made. He didn't want to get overexcited. It wasn't a sale yet. But the message was fantastic news. Typically, companies sent form letters thanking him for his interest and dismissing his submission as "not right for us at this time."

He ate two bowls of soup while watching *Jeopardy!* He fingered his classical guitar. He revised the lyrics of the mobile-home-park jingle. He washed dishes. He considered calling Meredith, but remembered that she and the baby would be out to dinner with her parents.

Gary went into the basement and with some difficulty located an empty box in the mountain of storage. There was no telling if Sally would be coming over tonight. He brought the box upstairs, gathered every framed photo in the house – nine in total of the family, the wedding, Barrett – and stacked them inside it. Gary hated the pictures of Barrett. He made a point of not looking at them. He slid the box into the bedroom closet.

At 7:00 PM Gary went to Messiah's to meet his coworker, Sally Vassar. He dropped seventeen quarters into a machine and received a pack of Camels. Over the next three hours, five pitchers of beer were drunk, and the cigarettes were smoked. Sally flirted while they shot pool. Gary didn't encourage her flirtation but offered subtle glances to let her know it was allowed.

A week earlier, to Gary's shock, Sally had been hired at Boogie. He hadn't seen her in fourteen months and had hoped to never see her again.

As they shot pool, questions formed in his mind: Why had she applied at Boogie? Why had she asked him to the bar? He kept wondering if he should make an excuse to drive her home, tell her "Thanks, but no thanks," and start searching for another job.

At nine-thirty, they were out of cigarettes. They left Messiah's.

They opened the door to Gary's house and were hit by the smell of diapers and baby wipes. Gary felt embarrassed that he'd hidden the pictures. He turned on the lights and showed Sally around, pointing at knick-knacks and explaining their significance to "me" (always using first person singular). Sally listened politely for twenty minutes. Then she curtseyed and asked if he would be so kind as to take her jacket.

After sex, it was an hour before sunrise. Sally slept atop the covers. Gary climbed out of bed. He went to the bathroom and scrubbed with liquid soap.

Increasingly, Gary worried that Meredith would find out about his affairs, or that some grisly misfortune would strike their baby. As an ex-Catholic branded by tenth-grade Latin, Gary knew that the prefix "ex" meant both "out of" and "from." This implied that he *consisted of* Catholicism as well as *used to be* Catholic. Like cells, Catholicism composed him. He would know no forgiveness unless he confessed, and yet a confession would destroy the life that was the very reason he had sinned in the first place. It was all very complicated.

Gary took a towel from the linen closet and dried himself. He urinated in a heavy stream with one palm pressed against the wall. The sex with Sally had been rote. If he was being honest, it had been nauseating. It was his fault. Sally was just a girl who liked to joke and have sex. She had no sinister intentions. She had no idea that he had turned their meaningless fling into a baby boy. Even Gary, at times, doubted it.

Standing at the toilet like this, eyes closed, Gary felt he might fall asleep, prick in hand, and never wake up.

A low moan floated up from the bathroom vent. The skin hardened on Gary's arms.

The moan sounded again, softly, conveying not physical pain but the patient misery of depression. It sounded like a man. Gary felt sure it was coming from the basement, or possibly the neighbor's backyard. Gary refrained from flushing and stepped out of the bathroom.

Tentative daylight filled the hallway. He heard the moan again, but this time from the bedroom, and this time not a man. The paperman's station wagon roared from the street. Gary opened the bedroom door. He paused at the threshold to confirm, absolutely, that no noise was coming from the basement.

"*Are you in or out?!*" Sally yelled.

"In," Gary answered.

He woke at 12:58 PM, alone. He stared at the ceiling, entertaining the idea that last night had been a dream. Gary rolled over and searched the pillowcase for signs – a smudge of lipstick or black hair dye. Only Sally's aroma lingered, like fresh-baked cookies that had been smoked on.

Gary brewed coffee. He telephoned Boogie. He told "Donnie" Donald that he couldn't work because of some nasty diarrhea. "Might be food poisoning," Gary said. Donnie was a corpulent old scenester who had played bass in one of Cincinnati's first punk bands. Donnie reminded Gary, "It is currently two hours *after* the start of your shift," but then added that business was slow anyway, and they probably wouldn't need him.

Then Donnie said, "Can you put Sally on for a sec?"

"Why would Sally be here?" Gary said.

Donnie mumbled incomprehensibly to someone nearby him. He returned to the line and told Gary he'd see him tomorrow. The line clicked dead.

Gary felt his head heating. Kevin, Charlie, Markus, Donnie – all the Boogie employees were now probably talking about the new in-store hook-up, even without the luxury of proof. Why the need to know everyone's business? Didn't people understand that gossip had consequences? Such talk had come dangerously close to Meredith's ears in the past, but Gary had killed each affair before she found out.

Or maybe she *had* heard. At times, it was tough to believe Meredith was in the dark. Before leaving town for ten days, their longest stretch ever, her parting words were: "Behave." How else could he interpret such a command? And yet if she knew about the affairs, why would she stay with him? Day after day, she presented a happy face. She hugged and kissed him as if nothing was wrong.

Coffee in hand, Gary went into the nursery after noticing that the blinds were open. He could see into the B&B next door. Miss West was visible, standing rock-still. A blind woman couldn't stare out a window, but that's what she appeared to be doing, squinting, a strip of sunlight fallen across her face. Her Amish-style dress and unshapely figure made her look like a potato. Her neck was red with acne or rash. The wispy hair atop her head would have scattered under a hairdryer.

She was fortunate, Gary thought, not to be able to see a mirror.

"Gary!"

He jumped. Coffee scalded his foot. Turning, he saw Sally in the rocking chair where Meredith did her nightly breastfeeding.

"You are a *zombie*," she said.

"I thought you left." His heart rattled his ribs.

"I forgot my pills."

"Try the doorbell next time."

Sally stood and exited. Gary heard the slam of the bathroom door. Sally was twenty-two, and her immaturity, he recalled now, had a tendency to reveal itself in painful ways. Using his bare hand, Gary wiped coffee from his toes. Sally shouted a melody through the house: "There's a lake of stew and of whiskey, too! You can paddle all around 'em in a big canoe, in the Big Rock Candy Mountain!"

★

She left a few hours later, after sex. This time, during an intense moment, she had pulled his face close and said, "I could fall in love with you."

He hissed at her, and nothing more was said. He had also lost his erection, but he made a big show of pretending to climax. Sally's comment stuck in his mind. Obviously, she hadn't meant it. She had gotten caught up in the moment. Or, more likely, she was messing with him, knowing that her remark would make him think about her while he had plenty of more important things on his mind.

It was 4:00 before he returned the Spad's Pizza call. Gary scolded himself. A lax attitude would never cut it in this business. Media Marketing Specialist Daniel Bruce, however, didn't seem to notice.

"We dig your jingle," he said. His voice was forceful. "But I need to ask how married you are to the lyrics."

"Well," Gary said, taken aback by the question but more by the groaning he was now hearing from the basement. "I think my lyrics are good."

"No one said your lyrics aren't good, Gary. But good isn't what we shoot for. Aim for the sun, hit the moon. We're after *outstanding*. Your tune is nice, but the verbiage needs to reflect the Spad's philosophy. Check out our website if you haven't. We aren't a trough. We don't want face-feeders. Face-feeders stop at the first shiny sign that doesn't require a left turn. We want *dreamers*. Chuck E. Cheese's, Domino's, Papa John's, Pizza Hut, Sbarro's, Little Caesars – you've heard of them? The top six pizza chains have 15,000 locations in the continental U.S. alone. You're probably wondering how we can possibly chisel into this monopoly. Answer: STAND OUT. . . ."

Gary walked toward the basement door while Mr. Bruce talked. On his way through the kitchen, Gary drew a knife from the block. He had heard two moans – distant, muffled, and unmistakably male. He pressed the Rec Conv button on the receiver.

"Got a pen?" Mr. Bruce said.

"Better," Gary said. "I'm recording this on my answering machine." He stepped onto the landing and descended the cement stairs. If there was a lunatic, best to confront him while someone else was within earshot.

"Fantastic. We need to axe the 'Never cold and never doughy/ Comes out quickly never slowly' line. Two reasons. First: we don't tell them what their pizza *won't* be. Two: we don't open up our kitchen. We aren't Subway. Three: too specific. The *everyman*, buddy. That's our market. People want abstract. Family, love, convenience. The quickness idea – great. Keep it. But. . . ."

At the bottom of the steps, in near-darkness, Gary heard the moan again. It was thin, animal-like. Maybe a wounded opossum. Gary stepped forward until he located the light string. He pulled.

"Mister and Missus Average American do not want in-the-box thinking," Daniel Bruce was saying. "That's a statistically proven fact. . . ."

The basement consisted of one large, damp room. The only hiding place for an intruder was amidst the unruly arrangement of boxes, lawn equipment, and suitcases in the west corner.

"We also need to do something with 'Goes down easy, never greasy.' We don't want our customers thinking about grease, do we, Gary? I'm just asking. I'm no Mick Fleetwood. It's not in me. I can tell you that 94% of Americans eat pizza, and that 350 slices go down 350 throats each *second* of each *day*, but don't ask me to write words about it."

Gary had surveyed the storage and was now relaxing because there didn't appear to be an intruder in or around it. A stack of boxes by the wall had toppled. He must have caused this yesterday when retrieving the empty box.

Daniel Bruce ended the conversation abruptly. He wanted notification as soon as Gary finished the revision; he was eager to "take it to the next level." As Gary hung up, he told himself he would review the tape later, transcribe Mr. Bruce's instructions, get a rewrite out by –

Ohhhhhhh.

The moan was a few feet away. At this distance, it sounded cheap and mechanical. Gary set the phone on the floor and searched through the toppled boxes, dragging them away from the wall. Among notebooks, graduation caps, a worn Nerf football, and high-school yearbooks, he found a baby doll the size of a premature infant. Gary picked it up. When Gary took it into his hands, it emitted a deep, plaintive groan.

Sally returned that evening, uninvited.

Gary had brought the doll upstairs and opened the battery casing on its rear end with a tiny Philips screwdriver. How the corroded, flaking AAs had succeeded in producing sound from this four-year-old toy was a mystery. Possibly they'd been jarred when the boxes tipped, causing some latent electric juice to surge. Gary removed the batteries and threw them in the trash, staining his fingertips orange.

The baby doll had been a gag gift at Meredith's bachelorette party. She and Gary had opted for co-ed bachelor and bachelorette parties. Old traditions, they believed, were sexist. They weren't going to launch a marriage partnership by perpetuating gender stereotypes. Meredith's mother, it turned out, was keen on having a grandchild. Surrounded by their friends and family, Meredith's mother Iris, a little wood-carving of a woman with bright blue eyes and a tan that seemed perpetually on the verge of turning like lunchmeat, said, "You might as well get some practice in before the real thing. Grandma says!" People cheered, but with an edge, as if a taboo topic had been broached. Everybody liked the idea of a baby, but they weren't sure how the not-yet-married couple would react to this physical embodiment of the concept. Gary and Meredith weren't offended by "Grandma's" provocative present. They wanted a child. Meredith shook her head and said, "You're such a mom, Mom," and playfully burped the doll before tossing it onto the pile of gifts.

Two years of trying ended with the conclusion that Gary was effectively infertile; "a 98% certainty" that he could not impregnate Meredith. "A 98% certainty" – the doctor's phrase was preposterous, and Gary joked about it darkly for the next few weeks. But it was devastating news. Since his father's death, Gary had dreamed of having a child. He'd convinced himself that it was his destiny to become the dad that his own dad had wanted to be. Gary heard the diagnosis with the realization that he had wasted his life on a fantasy.

Adopting a healthy newborn would require years of waiting, thousands of dollars, and paperwork that neither Gary nor Meredith felt inspired to complete. Fertility clinics cost far too much; they were already in debt from the consultations and tests. Gary and Meredith avoided each other around the house. Gary started what he thought would be a brief affair with Sally Vassar, a yoga instructor who worked at the IGA.

He and Sally had met by chance at a nearby bar and ended up at her apartment. Over the next month, they had sex five more times. Once a week, on weekends, Gary sneaked out after Meredith went to bed and walked to Sally's. Gary now understood that the Maker's Mark he and Sally downed each time had been used to hide the fact that they didn't actually like each other.

Sally had boasted that she hated commitment. She was openly sleeping with two other men. The flavored body jellies, nipple clamps, porno tapes, and handcuffs in her bedroom attested to her claims. Gary always made sure to wear a condom. After their fourth encounter, however, he had an unsettling idea.

Through conversation, Gary had learned that Sally used the pill with her other partners. Feigning jealousy, he quizzed Sally about them – their build, dress, hair color. At home, he researched on the Internet how long sperm could live inside a woman and also outside the body: Three days inside a woman and twenty-four hours outside, although opinions differed. In theory, he could transport a donation to Meredith and give them the baby they desired. The idea was repulsive if he thought much about it, so he didn't think about it. He didn't ponder the details. He concentrated on the idea of a baby, and the more he did so the more he felt like he was being creative and resourceful, finding a way around the bad luck of his biology.

Four nights later, Gary staked out Sally's apartment. From his parked car he watched a gangly, leather-clad kid in combat boots step up to the door and press the buzzer. After two hours, the kid left. Gary hopped out of his car and paid Sally a surprise visit without using a condom. Then he rushed home to Meredith.

Gary hated thinking about Sally Vassar, but these days, he couldn't help it.

*

Sally rang his doorbell at 6:00 PM. She was holding two brown grocery sacks and insisted on cooking dinner. She had walked all the way over, she said. Gary let her in. She made enchiladas in the kitchen while Gary reviewed Daniel Bruce's answering machine instructions and took notes. The sizzling air smelled like spiced beef. A Buzzcocks album played in the living room. When Sally finally served his enchilada, Gary could only eat three bites.

Sally was unhappy. Her face under the forty-watt bulbs – mushroom-colored skin, dark crescents beneath eyes brimming with calculated mania – provoked him. By the time they finished the second bottle of merlot, Sally was calling him an untalented loser, a shitty husband, and a snob. She said his wife deserved to know what a pig she was married to. Gary prayed she wouldn't hurl the pottery. He succeeded in calming her only after agreeing to let her write lyrics for the Spad's jingle. "You'll do it better than me, anyway," he said. Daniel Bruce wanted abstractions, and Gary couldn't do abstractions. He was stuck in the dirt and the muck and that was all he could see and he was choking on it. Sally stomped into the nursery with a notebook and pen.

Gary took the phone into the bedroom and called Meredith. He wanted to talk to Barrett, to say he was sorry. Barrett wouldn't understand a word, but this wouldn't change the fact that Gary had said it. The answering machine at Meredith's parents' house engaged; it was after midnight.

Gary hung up. He curled on the bed. On certain days he had laughed at the notion that he'd impregnated Meredith in such a vile way. Was it even possible? Surely the fertility doctor had been wrong. Surely Barrett was his boy, all his. But then doubt would return, and worse than doubt – the reality that he would never know the truth.

The faraway moan of the baby doll reached Gary's ears. It was an uncanny mixture of man, infant, and machine. Gary remembered removing the batteries.

He found Sally in the nursery, in the rocking chair. The notebook and pen lay on the floor. Some words were scribbled on the page. The doll was cradled in her arms.

"Get out of this room," Gary said.

"Our baby needs food," she laughed, positioning the doll's mouth at the breast she had exposed by removing a bra strap. "He feels neglected!"

Gary yanked her elbow. "I took the batteries out of that thing."

"What's your problem?"

"Go." He pointed at the nursery door, wishing he could indicate the front door from this vantage point.

"Awww. That chair is sacred. I understand. What a sweet man."

He pushed Sally out of the room. In the neighboring house Miss West sat in a recliner, bathed in television light, her expression grim and severe. Whether her eyes were open or closed, Gary couldn't tell.

After the fourth bottle of wine, Gary lost his physical coordination and speech. Days later, at Sally's funeral, he would recall impressions: arm-wrestling; an infomercial for a home dolly; a session of cold enchilada gorging; numerous crying jags. At some point, he passed out on the bed. He was wakened at 5:00 AM, fully clothed, by the baby.

*

At first he thought the moaning was Barrett. Meredith sometimes brought Barrett into bed to nurse.

Sally lay beside him. She was clear-eyed and drunk. The baby, positioned between her and Gary, moaned.

"Hey, baby doll," Sally said. "You hungry, baby doll? Too bad your mommy and daddy aren't here." She stroked the doll's stomach. "Who *is* your daddy? Nobody knows."

Gary grabbed the doll and threw it into the corner. "Get out," he said, "and don't come back." He was afraid if she stayed he might beat her. Who was she? Some nympho. She'd probably given him a disease. For all he knew she had stalked him to the record store to seduce him away from his family.

He drifted back to sleep. When he realized, minutes or hours later, that Sally was still in the bed, he shoved and kicked her. He didn't open his eyes. She fought back, but Gary was stronger. She fell off the mattress. She screamed profanities then stomped into the hallway. The front door slammed.

He awoke later to sirens.

*

Daniel Bruce congratulated Gary and said a contract was in the mail, along with the check. They hadn't expected such a major rewrite, but they couldn't be happier. Mr. Bruce made it clear that they weren't necessarily going to *use* Gary's jingle in a commercial – they were still considering a few others – but they were happy to buy the rights just in case. Gary hung up and stared at the floor.

Meredith helped him celebrate. They ordered Tikka Saag and tandoori chicken from the best Indian restaurant in town.

Meredith said she always knew it was a matter of time. They bought champagne and made love, and Barrett didn't disturb them with his cries.

The next day, the contract arrived. Gary signed and dated on the lines. Meredith joked about framing the two-thousand-dollar check.

Gary shrugged. "They probably won't even record it. They're essentially paying me so no one can hear it."

"They bought your song," Meredith said. "It means you're on your way, and it means we have a cushion."

"I don't want people to hear it anyway. The lyrics are rotten."

An hour later, someone knocked on the front door. Meredith poked her head into the bedroom to tell Gary that the police wanted to talk to him.

Two uniformed cops stood in the living room browsing the family photos and record albums. Each had forty pounds and five inches on Gary. They took turns squeezing his hand as if it were a stress-relief ball. Officer Baines told Gary to have a seat. Gary chose the recliner, un-reclined. Officer Baines took the couch while Officer Briggs stood with arms crossed in the center of the room. A black plastic bag dangled from Officer Briggs's hand. Its contents could not be discerned. Meredith, cradling Barrett, stood in front of the picture window.

"We need to ask a few follow-ups about the accident that took place last week," Officer Baines said. He produced a pen and note pad, which he opened to a blank page. "We're trying to determine if the driver behaved negligently. Officer Briggs says your original statement isn't very coherent."

Gary glanced at Officer Briggs, realizing this was the same cop who had questioned him while he stood staring at Sally Vassar's broken body on the pavement. It felt like a dream now.

"What accident?" Meredith asked.

The officers waited for Gary to answer.

"While you were at your parents', a young woman was hit by the paperman's station wagon," Gary said. "She died."

"Jesus," Meredith said. She looked stricken. "And you didn't tell me?"

"I didn't want to upset you."

"She was Gary's coworker," Officer Baines said to Meredith. "Right, Gary?"

"I already gave that information," Gary said.

"Then you know she lived four blocks from here."

"I don't know where my coworkers live."

"Any idea why she was running into the street in front of your house at six in the morning?"

Gary said no.

Officer Briggs was apparently in charge of stare-downs, which he performed while Officer Baines asked another question: "You went to the young woman's funeral. You were close?"

"Everyone from the record store went."

Baines flipped through his notebook. "So you two weren't close? I'm confused. Didn't you go to Messiah's bar with her the night before her accident?"

Meredith wasn't looking at Gary. She was studying Barrett in her arms as he indulged peacefully in his pacifier.

"She invited me," Gary said. "Coworkers go out all the time."

"Sounds fun," Baines said, offering some kind of smile. "And on the morning of the accident, you said you came out of the house because the sirens woke you."

"They scared me," Gary said. "I have a new baby, obviously." He nodded weakly in the direction of his child. "Hard to get into a deep sleep these days. You know how it is."

"I'll get to the point," Baines said. "Was Sally Vassar inside this house at any time before the accident?"

"She's never been in this house," Gary said.

"Your neighbor Miss West says she heard noise and yelling on the night before the accident."

Gary waved at the wall of records. "I like my music loud. I hope I didn't disturb her."

Briggs, who had been standing stoically, stepped forward while pulling an object out of the black bag. He set the object with a *clunk* on the coffee table. It was the baby doll, sealed in clear plastic and marked with EVIDENCE tape. "We found this on the street ten yards from Miss Vassar's body. Her fingerprints are all over it."

"Is there some point to these questions?" Meredith said. "The girl is dead and buried, isn't she?"

"We're trying to see the whole picture," Baines said. "If the girl was behaving erratically, we need to know. The driver is facing vehicular homicide charges."

The baby doll appeared undamaged – a bit soiled, perhaps – and it made no sound.

"Have you ever seen that station wagon driving recklessly?" Baines asked.

Gary thought for a moment. He wanted to look at Meredith but didn't dare. "I can't say I have."

"You, ma'am?"

"Never," Meredith said.

"But the doll came from this house – isn't that right?"

Gary was having trouble breathing; the air felt like syrup. He knew that he needed to speak up, to confess that Barrett was no more his son than this doll was, but no words came. In the corner of his eye, Meredith had become a shadow against the picture window.

"Do you think we'll find your fingerprints on the doll, Gary?" Officer Gaines said.

"I don't like what you're insinuating," Meredith said. "*My* fingerprints are probably on that stupid thing." Her tone was aggressive, as was her gesture when she lifted her shirt, unsnapped her nursing bra, and began feeding the baby. "I think it's pretty obvious what happened. Gary threw the doll on the curb with the rest of the garbage, and this girl, this dead girl, wandered by on the sidewalk and trash-picked it before she got run over." Meredith turned to Gary and offered a flat, determined stare. "Isn't that right?"

Gary loved his wife intensely in that moment, and he thought how beautiful and white she looked as she pressed the small boy's face to her chest under the scrutiny of the sun.

The Art of the Dead

I CHALK HER CORPSE INTO THE DIMPLED PAVEMENT UNDER
Hell's heat lamp, where no cars dare pass on this day. Her
angelic death, my final version this *Backless Corpse (Un)
Dressed*, I work toward until my bicep is tight and my shoulder
burns. Chalk to pavement, I push and grind like I'm sanding
skin, then pucker my lips, *puff puff*, and scatter colored dust
with rum breath. When my sweat makes puddles, I blend the
red, green, and yellow pools with my fingertip. The sun bites
my shirtless back. It must be afternoon, and I must be a piece
of bacon. Or a piece of shit, if you ask the dead, or the Dad for
that matter, although to the Dad I *am* one of the dead, more
worthless than a piece of shit because at least shit will fertilize.

I keep working (How much time has passed? Fuck time.),
working through the pain.

Joe and Judy college professor throw their shadows onto
coloring book chalkings that give them orgasms. Mabel and
Marty khaki shorts with athletic socks punish me with their
children's squeaky voices (mice with broken spines pinned to
wooden slats). Grandma and Grandpa pension plan glide like
clouds past my *Backless Corpse (Un)Dressed* for reasons I care
nothing about. I only see the pits in the pavement. I only chalk.

Then, the inevitable:

"What's this one, Mommy-Mom? It's a funny bunny colory-color."

"Umm . . . That's a . . . What? *Oh my*. Avert your eyes, Billy. Avert them with the aid of my hand, or your brain will liquify and drain out of your ears."

"That looks like a donut."

"Billy, for the love of humanity come with Mommy, come away from the man with the gnarled teeth and bird's-nest hair who is so out of his mind that he doesn't even notice that his knees are blistered because he's so wrapped up in drawing a naked woman's corpse, behavior that is both repulsive and strangely compelling and might make me leave your father for a life of wild-dogging I've never gotten at home. . . . COME, BILLY! BEFORE HE TURNS YOU INTO AN ART LOVER."

Yes, go Billy. Go before I drag my lobstered body to the curb, light my cigarette, and allow your 2,000-day-old eyeballs to view in uncensored grandeur the lifelessness that awaits even Christian soldiers like you and your sweet, under-penetrated mother. Go, Billy, to the other lane of the street. Dance around the colorful vomit stain of chalk that more or less resembles a tree, a river, and a bridge with a cat on it, and which was created, if you can call it that, by Greta VanDerBilmenn, Judge Garrett VanDerBilmenn's long-legged only daughter, who before today has never created anything other than one shredded heart, thousands of Dentyne bubbles, and a pair of amateurish renderings of an unplugged computer monitor. Enjoy Greta's super-sized vapidity, because I have no time for you, and she has no moving blood in her veins.

Meanwhile, I am living my wedge – this baby blue wedge – into her lips.

"Excuse me."

This man's voice is not for me. It can't be. Blue. Puff the blue dust. Scatter it. Puff.

"Sir? SIR?! Jasper Goodwin, I am required to talk to you? I'm Burt Farmer, Head Executive Director Chairman of the Street Art Panel Committee Board for the Artistic Advancement of Street Chalk Artists and Their Fellow Artists' Art."

I lift my face to the retina-scorching sun. Somewhere up there, a shrimpy shadow inspects me.

"You are required to change this drawing," he says. "You are Jasper Goodwin, aren't you?"

No need to answer. It's a rhetorical question.

"Say," he chuckles. "You're not related to Jessup Goodwin II, founder of Goodwin's Laser Plastic Surgery Institute in Grand Rapids, Michigan, are you? I really wouldn't ask (judging by your hair, flip-flops, and odor, you and he are as different as butter and milk), except you do resemble the Great God Goodwin in profile. He and I shared box seats at the Chicago Opera House in 1992 for a performance of the three tenors, while his wife was still bravely battling the cervical cancer that eventually – "

Enough.

I yell at the cement, hoping my words will bounce upward, hit me in the face, give me amnesia: "Call me President Drone Grunt Clock-Watcher of Dead Beauties Incorporated, established two days after the one-time loving of the woman in this chalking, sir!"

My outburst snaps him out of his reminiscence of a woman he doesn't deserve to have known: "I'll have none of your bull, Mr. Goodwin. You can't leave this artwork the way it is."

"I don't intend to. I'm going to finish her."

By puffing his chest, Mr. Whomever throws his machismo

into the air, where it dances away like a sheet of fabric softener on the breeze. "You're planning to put some clothes on this thing?"

This "thing" is the woman who hugged me to her naked bosom so many times (okay, only once, but for many seconds) during her brief life.

By contrast, this shrimp, this seven-thousandth slave of the Judge, this coincidental lacky to Laser Plastic Surgery Barons, this delicate (slouching under the weight of the soft briefcase slung over his shoulder) who mistakes power with the ability to crush a cardboard Pepsi cup in his fist, knows nothing of the ways art can both destroy and resurrect a human life.

His beard is red, twinkly, spooged-on by the sun. "We've had eleven complaints, Mr. Goodwin. I'm not sure what sort of family you grew up in, but families here do not wish to view filth. Your cartoon doesn't come close to the sketch the Board approved, which, conveniently, is here in my hand. *This* is a unicorn." He points at the joke I mailed to the Advisory Board last week under the influence of King Cobra, depression, and Costbusters baked beans. "*That*, Mr. Goodwin?" His finger droops like a dead caterpillar.

The corpse's flesh form, meanwhile, stands across the street in the shaded gap between Tink's Café and the brownstone, pulverizing her Dentyne, peering surreptitiously to make sure her portrait artist is skillfully, and with an abundance of humiliation, destroyed. She sees me seeing her for the first time today, even though we've been coloring the same pavement since 9:00 AM. Her eyes are vivid even at thirty feet distance. That bright, watery life. How could I recreate it, if I ever had to, on this scabrous surface? It's a good thing she, and others, are dead with their lids closed. If I had to capture her eyes in life, I'd need more than chalk. I suspect I've known this all along, which is why I waited, like I always do, until she passed away.

"Mr. Goodwin!"

Then, "Mr. Goodwin!"

Then, "Mr. Goodwin!"

And so on.

A few minutes later, the annoying man is gone, and Cheyenne Lovely's bare toes are an inch from my face.

"You've got guts," she says.

I keep chalking. I'm nearly finished.

"They're coming back, you know," she says. "But I'm behind you. It's bullshit."

A final touch-up on the collarbone, one last trip to the appendix scar . . . it is complete. I'm a pile of sore flesh with pebbles lodged in my knees, ready to witness my creation. I push myself from the pavement, rise.

"Wow wow wow. It's amazing," Cheyenne says. She lays her bare arm across my shoulders.

I scream. "AAAAAAHHHHHHH!!!!!!!"

She apologizes in four languages, rubs lotion over my burns. We smoke her cigarettes on the curb and talk about *My Dead* (my new, more accurate, more inclusive title), all eleven feet of her: majestic breasts, placid face, fluffy flower vagina. Cheyenne calls it disturbing and primitive.

We turn our heads and see a guy dragging a hose toward us. He's a black fellow with close-cut hair and a fuzzy mustache. In his green jumpsuit I don't recognize him until he winks at me. It's Montel. I give him a nod, feel the urge to hurl him to the ground, rifle through his pockets, and steal the limousine keys. He tells us: "Watch out." The nozzle is turned, and *My Dead* washes quietly into the sewer.

The other chalk drawers (*Dead* included), along with Joe and Judy college professor, Grandpa and Grandma pension plan, Marty and Mabel athletic socks with khaki shorts – and yes, even the hydrant-sized victims (the children, with uneven haircuts) – stare and lick their lips while the street bleeds.

Cheyenne puts her face on my shoulder. I absorb the pain. *My Dead* is melting, melting, melted. I want a burrito, and I want out of here, because my living *Dead* is no longer standing between the buildings.

★

Cheyenne and I feed our faces at the Latin American place down the block. She's a describer: in literary detail her love of urban art ("Graffiti is so meaningful"); her disdain for the design academy that flunked her ("for political reasons"); her happiness at breaking her poverty-induced diet of rice cakes fried in cinnamon butter (she actually sold a drawing to some blind man); and finally, touchingly, her intense description of the clinging curl of spiced beef in my beard.

"I've seen you around," she says. She tweezers the beef with her thumb and finger, offers it to my lips.

"Not surprising," I say, chewing. "I'm around."

"Everyone knows who you are."

But how do I know you, Cheyenne Lovely? Have I listened to the tinkles of your ankle bells as you answered the call of the coffee shop ladies' room? Have I overheard your name mouthed by your gaggle of college-dropout friends? Have I noted your furrowed brow as you chatted on your phone? Have I internalized such visions while I pondered, oh so uncomfortably, what level of familial privilege might allow your sub-rudimentary art to "sustain" you?

She says: "I could never ever draw like you. I can see the thing in my head, but it comes out all wrong."

"See it other ways."

"I try to see it with my heart."

"I meant your goddamn eyes." I suck down the Corona, exacting my small revenge on the sun. "Buy me another."

She does. Then she does again. And again. We get drunk and full on her dime. I'm belching into my hand. Her hairy calf is making friends with mine. "I'm peaking," she tells me.

"I'm way too much for you," I tell her.

She pouts like a phony.

"Fine," I say.

★

Number 17 takes us to Over the Rhine, where buildings are burnt matchbooks. In the entryway of my brownstone an empty (got to lift and make sure) forty-ouncer stands on the floor in a sack under the row of metal mailboxes. The compulsion to return the bottle rages impotently, even after a decade in Ohio.

Turns out I don't need the dime (that I wouldn't get anyway) anyway. It's pay(off)day! My bulging baby boy, the 5x7 manila envelope in my mailbox, gives me, as usual, a hard-on. But Cheyenne doesn't even question the fatty I withdraw before her eyes so giddily. She leads me up the steps. I follow behind, rip the "Notice to Quit/ Nonpayment of Rent" off the #202 door, key us inside.

I tack the notice on the wall beside three other lovely notices. Lovely notices. She sees words where I see only black lines. "You'll get evicted," she warns. "It happened to my sister last month."

Maybe she wants to be a hero, pay my rent. Maybe she's already in love.

I tell her to lose the clothes if she wants to be captured. She drops them, drops glances. My duds join hers on the carpet. She is patchouli-fragrant, the age of an infant if I call myself twenty-one. We walk into my bedroom, two nude binaries.

She screams, "*They're everywhere.*" It's a quiet one, a whispered one, but still a scream – of wonder, awe, ecstasy.

She means my *Dead* drawings – wallpaper, carpet, bed-spread, clutter, snowfall. Fourteen minutes of sexual bliss had inspired chalking like never before, ten pieces a day. I dripped as much blood and plasma as the center would allow, visited the Kinko's, relieved a construction site of its staple gun, and began the Artistic Initiative for Spreading Beauty to the Uncul-tured Masses Via the Branchless Trees of the New Millennium. Even before the phlebotomist plunged his needle, I had tapped a vein for this art. It was too good, too important. I needed to let humankind touch it with its eyes.

Cheyenne's not frightened. These are windows into my pas-sion, and she wants me to know that she knows passion is a cool thing. She rolls in the drawings, whitewashes her flesh.

The telephone *brrrrings.* From the floor, Lovely frowns my walk to the nightstand. She wants to be more important than this call.

"Tell me something," I say into the receiver.

"Jasper Goodwin? Greta VanDerBilmenn here: long-legged chalk-artist daughter of Judge Garrett VanDerBilmenn and ad-mirer of all things colorful except, of course, you."

"I wish I could say this was unexpected."

"Cheyenne Lovely's in your bedroom?"

"Me as well."

"You're both nude?"

"Mostly," I say. My brown socks, feet intact, agree.

Cheyenne pretends she isn't eavesdropping. Warms herself by breaststroking in my art.

"Leave the phone off the hook so I can record it for poster-ity."

"Impossible. I'm burned over most of my body." I hang up.

"These portraits are haunting," Cheyenne says, seated on the carpet, holding *Treatment of a Future Corpse I* and *II*. (Two of my lamest from just after this *Dead* died, when Officer Billups gave me a warning most stern.)

Still, I didn't invite Cheyenne for her taste. Her eyebrows are untamed. Her legs, drawn up against her chest, are neglected by razor and treadmill. Teeth and gums don't fit in her mouth. In short, she's picture-imperfect. A living negative of a dead positive. Binaries again.

"Model for me," I say. I arm-sweep the bed, spread drawings across the floor like seeds atop other seeds. Cheyenne mounts my single mattress and sniffs the sheet. I grab the tin of chalk from atop the disconnected computer monitor, assume the stool, face the easel. Many thanks that my rear cheeks are un-kissed by the sun today.

"Legs," I tell her, gesturing.

"I've never modeled," she says. Her eyes are canisters of worry, fear, and hopes of string-free, acid-soaked sex with a local legend.

I swipe, swipe, swipe – my initial attack, my mountain-lion-on-the-sheep-of-the-canvas method, my decade-without-a-father fury – and the colors morph into an orderly nonsense before my eyes.

Lovely is on her back. Her pupils open like tiny throats as she addresses my ceiling: "I got Honorable Mention in last year's Street Drawing Chalk Festival for the Families of Recent-ly-Scorched Firemen." As if this will excuse her for the damage she and all of the other 'artists,' especially Greta, did to my eyeballs today.

Yours was a coyote portrait, and for that, Cheyenne, you should be mercilessly educated.

She believes we are engaged in foreplay, that this session will end with a slapping of damp groins, a few bowls of grass, and a shared gaze out the cracked bedroom window at whatever stars are strong enough to penetrate the forcefield of Cincinnati's lights. The phone rings. Her eyes study my mound of unwashed clothing, my caseless bugle tied to the corner by spider webs, my closet door off its hinges leaving visible the brown garbage bag within.

That stuffed garbage bag looks more like a fat lung every day.

The phone rings.

"I'm digging your ceiling," Cheyenne says. "The trick slopes up there. I feel like a total mustard ball."

The phone rings. I chalk. Smudge the shit brown of Cheyenne's hair, a chocolate shake upset on the mattress.

The phone rings. The phone rings.

Then my recorded voice, groggy and hateful: "If you are one of my dead, leave a message. If you are anybody else – "
Beeeeeeeeeeeeep!

"I'm already lost," comes the voice.

Bravo to that growl. I can taste it in my mouth.

Cheyenne flashes eyes at the machine.

The voice keeps coming: "I'm lost, and so are you, *Cheyenne Lovely.*"

Lovely bolts upright, covers her breasts with her arms.

Dead: "If you don't want to end up like me, you will get the fuck out of there! Now!"

Lovely's bewildered, broken expression is probably the same one I showed Dad when he killed me. Except Lovely's giving it to a telephone. She paws at the edge of the mattress for her clothes.

"I'm not through," I say.

"Go, Cheyenne! Get help! Find the police and bring them to his apartment!"

"Who is that?" Cheyenne's arms are bursting through her shirt sleeves. "How does she know my name?" Her skirt she wraps around her. Everything else – panties, sandals, bandanna, hipsack – is gathered into a hasty bundle.

Her second question is valid, although easily explained since Dead's father was on the committee that chose this year's chalkers, and since Dead, morbidly afraid of making public her love for me, couldn't prevent me from being selected (although to my shame she did stop me from immortalizing her by hosing my portrait into the drain) and was therefore within viewing distance when Cheyenne Lovely escorted me to my first burrito of the new millennium. Those goddamn burritos are not cheap. Lovely deserves better than this.

She arms herself with the lamp from the top of my dresser. She swings it. "Keep away!"

She runs from my room, face gray.

"He's done this before!" comes Dead. "Look under the floorboards!"

I pick up the phone. Uncradled, Dead's rant stops abruptly.

"She took my lamp," I tell the mouthpiece, "before I could tell her I love her."

"Enough screwing around, Blump. The Judge is in Boston, and Montel is on his way."

"You're dead," I say. "Officially. They – or you – even sent an underpaid African American man who bore a strange resemblance to Montel to hose you from the street, which means I am purged of you forever."

"Pack it all into a sack," she says, being carefully aggressive, or aggressively careful, like she's convincing a lion to eat a basket of cheeses. "Every drawing, doodle, napkin splotch, pencil sketch . . . every goddamn semen-stained blanket. I'll show you what a purging is."

I keep listening. It takes a few seconds to distinguish the dial tone from her voice. She's a demanding corpse just as she was a demanding lover.

Twenty minutes later (enough time to prepare), there's a buzz. I buzz back. Then the knock. Montel has swapped green jumpsuit for dashing three-piece suit. I'm happy to see him.

★

"What's your problem? You need to clean yourself up. It's a matter of personal pride. That ain't hairstyle, that's Grizzly Adams."

A lecture is what I get, from eyes in a mirror. No concern that a fellow human being's most sacred art project is crammed like common junk mail into a garbage bag. Not a care that the stench of leather interior makes me nauseous, or that my father pays me – like it's his vocation! – to stay out of his life.

"How bad do you want to go to jail?"

"I'm already there."

"That's offensive." His rear-view eyes shoot me. "I am personally offended by that statement. 'I'm already in jail.' If you were black, you'd be in jail last month. Pictures in a trash bag, getting off no problem. . . ."

"She loved me."

"Okay, you proved it. You need to be institutionalized."

Without Montel's scrutiny, I slide today's manila envelope out of my cutoffs' pocket. Open it. Two-thousand in fifties so new they could slice tomatoes. No note. Why would there be?

The silent stack says enough: *Keep out of Michigan. Do not attempt to contact me. Pay your rent and feed your bloated face. If you must self-destruct, do it under a different name.*

Ten years ago at the Kent County lock-up, Dad resembled a zoo visitor as he watched his $400 Italian leather Raffaellos get splattered by my withdrawal puke.

I open the garbage bag. In goes the stack of Grants. Seeds on top of seeds.

Montel is talking: "Listen to me, Jasper. YOU CANNOT KEEP FOLLOWING MISS VANDERBILMENN. Do you comprehend that? I'm trying to help you. I got three little girls. Financial pressures, all kinds of new shoes with lights on the soles, softball mitts. Lunchables, Munchables, Crunchables – no end to what crap I got to buy. When was the last time I paid more than four bucks for a six-pack of beer? You think that's fair?. . ."

It's not Montel's fault. The facts paint me as enemy. They're all he's paid to know – my name, for example, but not my NAME. He knows I'm a word-of-mouth chalk and charcoal legend in the Gaslight district of Cincinnati because Greta told him so after he limousined her affluent ass to the coffee shop on Ludlow two months ago so she could slum with the local color. He knows (he stood at her side) that Greta:

    1. spotted my *Fanciful Dagger Self-Portrait with "Bride"* series populating the coffee shop walls

    2. spotted my tank-top and beard (and the haunted loneliness in my eyes)

    3. spotted the work-in-progress on my lap

    4. practically begged me to give her lessons at forty bucks per half-hour.

(To her credit, tears did fill Greta's eyes, and she sniffled into her kerchief. She later blamed these secretions on seasonal allergies aggravated by smoke, but such an elaborate excuse couldn't hide the fact that she had recognized my most serious, most moving work: a series of portraits of my cancer-ridden, half-dead mother, begowned in traditional bridal garb and being given away, by me, to the skeletal, somber groom – the Grim Reaper himself – whose bone structure was modelled upon Daddy's, of course.)

Breaking into my sphere now and then:

"... She's the daughter of a *judge*? A fucker with a gavel? IT IS NOT MATH, MY FRIEND. He'll drop that hammer on your head if he knows you're stapling his naked daughter to telephone poles, creeping her out when she wants a manicure. ..."

One appraisal at the coffee shop and I thought that even my dreams wouldn't allow me to bed Greta. Her form, clothing, carriage – all were sickeningly familiar, as if my drawings had stepped off the walls. A life born of ridiculous advantage, in the flesh. Still, I agreed to teach her. Montel couriered her to the lessons. Like clockwork, my ears suffered the pleasurable *zzzzzzzzz* of the buzzer, the soft knock at my door. My eyes suffered her expensive eyebrows and aquiline nose. Thrice she wore the velour sweat suit that hugged her midriff and accentuated her jiggly little behind – only once the backless black dress in which she was buried. Ordered to remain in the hallway (leaning against the wall, tickling his cell phone), Montel never witnessed Greta's eyes floating upward to meet mine whenever my hand covered hers to demonstrate the swiping motion of the chalk.

On the fourth day of lessons, Greta seduced me on my bed, leaving me nauseous.

On the fifth, she called to cancel her lesson, citing a "blinding migraine."

On the sixth, Montel informed me by phone that Miss Van-DerBilmenn would no longer be needing my artistic services from now until Satan's warts were Nitroglycerined off his ass cheeks. Furthermore, that Miss VanDerBilmenn was requesting my utmost discretion in this matter, and that if a few hundred dollars would be necessary, such an amount could be procured. . . . I hung up on him.

*

The world stops rolling. A gate swings open. The limo crawls like a beetle up the driveway. Outside the tinted window is everything I imagined – golf course-like lawn, shrubs like rows of perfect teeth, distant grove of trees violated by a dirt path.

Our deepest desire is not that Heaven smells of fresh-cut grass but that it stinks of rotten apples.

I haul the trash bag to the mansion's front door.

"No chance," I warn Montel. He wants to take the bag.

First it's an *I'm-not-kidding* glare while we tug. Then he re-laxes, probably because although I'm a flabby guy with unruly body hair who possesses little in the way of combat training to compare to his security guard certificate and Tae Kwon Do orange belt, he knows I'll beat him on passion alone. I've never thrown a punch but also never received one.

Even Dad couldn't lay a hand on me. Even his two-million per-year laser surgery empire couldn't paddle me into Princeton, Harvard, Dartmouth, or any on his laundry list. Even his obese stock portfolio couldn't paddle me out of jail three times or out of a heroin enslavement followed by a series of heroine enslavements. The collection of drab landscapes marring his walls proved Dad's inability to truly see art (and also, therefore, with the slight extension of a fingertip, death).

"Blump," Greta says, smiling (but not sweetly, not like Mom) with a pistol pointed at my face (but not sweetly, not like Dad) when she opens the door.

"You're aiming wrong." I heft the garbage bag up to my chin.

"I tried to take it from him," Montel answers. "He's being uncooperative."

Her pistol becomes a maraca. "You had no cause to *hurt me*. Just because I showed a moment of weakness while I was in a fragile state after I got rejected by the University of Michigan thanks to reverse racial discrimination, you cannot prey on me. You have no idea what it's like to have a reputation and a future that is tied to that reputation."

Montel suggests that she lower the gun and eat a blueberry muffin. "Your blood sugar," he says.

She's wrong about my understanding of reputation. Reputation is precisely why I decided ten years ago to construct my life in chalk even if it meant food stamps, welfare checks, and stolen art supplies. Only occasionally have I sold my art. Five pieces in as many years. If I am honest, my legendary status is based upon my Sasquatchian beard and habitual street-roaming. I am everything my father hated. My failures are my success.

I am Jessup Goodwin III. I would tell Greta everything – who I am and who she is to me, and that it was a son's love that drew me to her – except there are body parts in my arms that need a proper burial.

I speak: "Greta VanDerBilmenn, a.k.a. *My Dead*, I certainly admit the possibility that I walked near you on public streets during a few of your trips to the post office, hair salon, bank, petting zoo, and workout gym. Perhaps I walked near you to an unlawful degree. But you must remember that you died to me those long weeks ago when you stopped caring about my artistic method. After that point, I was only doing research for the purposes of – "

"Give me the bag," she says.

"It's too heavy for you." (It weighs eleven pounds.)

"Give it to Montel."

"I won't."

She wants to evacuate my cranium, but instead she tells me to bring it inside. And in we go.

Hello, vestibule with unbearable cathedral ceilings. Greetings, vulgar spiral staircase and way-up-there windows that turn daylight into an overhead airplane which might or might not be worth craning to see. You are no different from Dad's house.

Greta leads me to living room, or parlor, or whatever she deems this soulless chamber.

"Drop it there."

Thirty-eight steps later I squat, depositing my treasure in front of the fireplace. I study the garbage bag, so full of something other than life. I lift my face to my Dead/Greta/Mother.

"The problem isn't me."

"You don't know when to shut up." Her voice is as hollow as the room. She cocks the gun with a *click*.

"We're water from the same faucet," I say. Forward steps. Leaving my brown lung alone within distance of the tongues.

"Cell phone, Montel," Greta says, "and dial *nine, one*. I'll tell you when to hit the other *one*. We've got an intruder. I have the right to blow his head off."

"Miss VanDerBilmenn, this dude is not violent. I got kids. I don't need bullets flying in the same room as me."

She turns on Montel. "Did *you* get stalked like a gazelle? Did you have to wonder if your father would discover you'd slept with a hobo?" She points the gun at the bag. "If my father knew about even *one* of those things, this asshole would never see the sun again."

"The judge," I say, my non-threatening trajectory bisecting Montel and Greta, bisecting the scarcely-furnished chamber, "passes judgment even when he declares your innocence. He sets his watch by your errors. I've met his kind before."

"Keep talking," she tells me.

I can't prove it, but I know she's leveling her gun at the back of my head. It feels good to be in somebody's sights.

I've visualized death many times in the past ten years. Perfumed, it stands behind you in the mirror. It helps you ride your bike without training wheels. It shows you how to straighten your bow tie for prom. Pink flowers from its kisses remain bloomed on your cheek even after you've gone AWOL from the Army, even after its lips turn blue.

I'll walk ten miles. My apartment may not be mine. Days will pass. I'll sleep, shit, and eat. Another envelope of art will find me, somehow. Another bag will begin its filling. I'll meet Cheyenne Lovely again. My chalk tin will open for her.

I feel free, floaty. My brains might come barfing out of my forehead. I might collapse, bleeding my epitaph across the marble. Montel mutters prayers.

It's my best work right there inside that brown lung, that bag stuffed with nearly 5,000 mini-canvases. Each canvas bears the stern patrician, the green-gray Grant who grants nothing but obedience. Found art, as they say. It found me.

Greta will open the garbage bag – there is no doubt – but will she recognize *My Dead*?

The Odds

MY GRANDMA HAD A BRAIN ANEURYSM THE OTHER WEEK WHILE peeling onions at the kitchen counter. Her reading glasses were on, but not to aid her vision. She has always maintained that the lenses deflect the onion fumes, keeping her crying to a minimum. I've heard conflicting opinions about this glasses/no glasses effect on onion tears, but this is the position my grandma maintained.

She lost consciousness with the knife in her hand. Luckily she didn't stab herself, but her face met the table as she collapsed. I was on the sofa. I heard the thud, heard the metallic skipping of eyeglasses across linoleum, and came running. The first thing I did was cover her legs. Her dress had bunched up on her hips, and with the stockings ending at the knees she looked weirdly salacious. I was uncomfortable; Grandma's mouth was bleeding. She convulsed. Her eyes had gone white.

After she got checked into the hospital, I kicked myself for not recognizing the warning signs. She'd been complaining of sharp headaches for a few weeks and occasionally saw two of Angela Lansbury on reruns of *Murder, She Wrote*. She'd been "misplacing" her keys when she had them in her hand. One morning she called me "Martin," the name of her son – my dad – who is ten years deceased.

When the intracerebral hemorrhage hit, it flooded her brain with blood. That's why she lost consciousness and fell. Her jaw (the mandible) broke when her face hit the table. The doctor – his name was Hillvan Socrates – gave me the diagnosis. He was a tall, thick, red-faced Greek, heavy on the eyebrows, who appeared to be approaching retirement age. He said they had done X-rays and I should be thankful she didn't have any spinal injuries in the neck, which sometimes happens when jaws crack.

He talked on for a few more minutes, pointing with his pen at a cutaway drawing of a skull with a brain inside it that was on some kind of easel-type thing next to his desk. His nostrils were formidable black holes – I imagined that with a well-positioned flashlight I could illuminate his own brain cavity and follow more closely what he was saying. Socrates said he could perform an operation to drain the blood, but at her age anything could happen. This meant, I assumed, that she had little chance of survival.

I'd been on a hot streak for the previous six months. Pool was my thing, mostly, though I wasn't a shark. I had what I thought was a pretty interesting angle, spending from nine until two every night at various bars simply watching people, drinking beer, getting a sense of who was a regular, who was a decent player, etc. Over time I'd cultivated a "winner" profile, an amalgam of physical attributes, clothing habits, hairstyles and whatnot. Winners had self-assured movements, controlled gestures. They stood up straight, didn't need to laugh at every attempted joke, sipped their drinks rather than guzzled. They weren't cocky, just precise in their expenditure of energy. I also had to consider the context of each situation – if there were two "loser" types together, obviously one of them would emerge victorious, and I had to calculate who was the lesser loser.

Then, when a couple guys squared off, I would lay fifty bucks on the table and say, "I think Johnny here's gonna win this one." If Johnny's opponent didn't want to bet, then fine. Usually he did.

This was my main source of income. I didn't win every time, but my success percentage stood at around eighty. Now and then, of course, I'd have the loser waiting for me in the parking lot, ready to fuck up my face, but I made a point of walking out with the winner so he could defend me. Some of the losers thought it was a big racket, that I was in cahoots with the other player, but usually they didn't because they had made the bet, they had lost, end of story. My face got pounded exactly two times in as many years. I considered this an acceptable rate of hazard.

Aside from the $500 a week or so I pulled in on the pool gig, I wagered on whatever people were willing to wager on. Here are some examples: I bet $25 that my buddy Earl couldn't walk across the living-room floor with an empty beer bottle on his head; I won $40 from a drunk at the local brewpub who insisted that Rush's *2112* was released before *A Farewell to Kings*. Miscellaneous things like that. My biggest score to date was from a Pfizer bigwig who frequented the golf club where I worked briefly as a caddy. He handed me six hundred smackers for missing a putt from four feet, three inches.

My eyes and ears are in a perpetual state of awareness; they are my bodyguards. There's a trancelike state, like a pre-orgasm masturbation feel, a tingle in my gut, when I can sense both a betting man and the circumstances in which to trap him.

Grandma was conscious in her hospital bed. She was understandably a little grumpy, but sporadically so because most of the time she was spaced-out from the drugs. My initial plan had been to feed her her meals, but of course her broken jaw prevented chewing. She was fed intravenously, so I did what I could: I sat beside her; I read to her from the newspaper; I held her hand. Her thought process, considering the saturated condition of her brain, seemed surprisingly cohesive, especially in short bursts. She asked about her bills, and I said not to worry, that I was taking care of things.

We'd been living together for eighteen months. She provided me with a comfortable house, hot meals, an address, some conversation. I made sure bills were paid, lightbulbs were functioning, mail made it into the house, and on and on. I think she appreciated my friendship as well. We liked each other in the same way an old dog and a tiny kitten will become chums. Our differences – in age, sex, experience, attitude, clothing style, diet – bonded us and made us protective of each other.

Grandma had outlived all of her children, which is tragic. Her youngest daughter, my Aunt Carla, died first from a freak case of pneumococcal pneumonia at nineteen. Next to go was my dad, Martin, at the age of fifty. He suffered a stroke, lived for eleven more months, and then passed quietly in his sleep.

Friends who know me well, know my family situation, have remarked that it's strange for someone like me, who has suffered many blows of "bad luck," to be such an avid gambler. I've never seen these things as "bad luck." They were just occurrences that affected a small group of people within a certain radius. I view life as a big pond, where it's raining. I'm in a certain area of the pond. The rain is what happens to me, what happens to people around me. Sometimes it sprinkles, sometimes it pours. The raindrops make ripples. We feel these ripples when they hit us, we feel turbulence. At times the ripples overlap so we're feeling turbulence compounded by other turbulence, but nobody feels *everything* that's going on in that pond. It's actually *good* luck that we don't.

At 10:30 PM I thought Grandma was asleep when she opened her eyes, looked at me, and said, "You hurt your foot. Poor darling hurt his foot." The skin surrounding her face bandage, what I could see of it, was the color of a rotten banana. Her cheeks were sagging so much that the bottoms of her eyeballs were exposed, like her face was melting off the bone. She went on a bit longer about my foot, in a near-inaudible whisper, then took a deep breath through her nose and said, "Poor little Wayne McClane."

My name isn't Wayne. Wayne was her middle child, my dad's younger brother. Our family name is not McClane. "Wayne McClane" was a nickname Grandma had given to Wayne when he was seven. It had something to do with a local sax player in a VFW band who Wayne was the spitting image of. Folks used to tease Grandpa that Wayne wasn't really his boy.

It gets more complicated when you realize that my mother, four years before my father's death, ran away with Wayne to Portland, Oregon. It was a big family scandal, for which my mother has never apologized. I believe she would say that it's impossible to know the human heart and that if the heart directs you to do something, it can't be wrong. Quite possibly she views her heart as a separate being, some kind of Siamese twin capable of making its own decisions, decisions which – unfortunately! – affect her. It's her heart; she knows it better than the rest of us. Anyway, Wayne's ship came in two years after my father's, in the form of colon cancer. It ripped through him in a matter of months, and then Grandma had no more children. My mother is still alive.

★

Grandma's surgery was scheduled for Wednesday morning. It was Monday evening when she called me "Wayne McClane." Doctor Socrates sat me down in his office at midnight and explained the operation. His fingers were hairy, and he was fond of plucking at the hairs. They were going to make a hole in Grandma's head, stick a tube inside, and drain out the blood. The broken jaw had exacerbated the flow of blood into the brain. Her condition was not dire, he said, but tenuous. It was a risky operation, even for someone in good health, so Grandma's chance of survival sat in the murky area of 25%.

I shook his hairy hand up and down and thanked him, then left. Back at Grandma's, I smoked about twenty-five cigarettes. She didn't allow smoking in her house. I'd never broken this rule before, but I was stressed. Her house felt like a cave, quiet and oppressive. A dog barked outside the entire night.

★

I had to bet on Death. I had no choice. If I'd bet on Life, then Doctor Socrates would have had a vested interest in botching the surgery. I'm not implying that he would have, but in any case it would've been much tougher to convince him to participate. Besides, I had two other, very valid reasons for betting on Death: 1) I'd pegged Socrates as a loser, and 2) I knew about odds, and the Lawrence family had never beaten them.

On Tuesday morning I caught Socrates in the hallway at St. Mary's and invited him out for a drink that night. He balked at first, as I knew he would. Even an innocuous thing like socializing with a patient's relative probably either violated some ethical code or, at the least, felt like a violation. But I can be persuasive when I need to be, and I could see in his hunched step, his heavy jowls and bag-bearing eyes, that he needed a break from his life. I pestered him until he relented.

We met at a sports bar. I barely recognized him without the white coat and clipboard. He was encased in an argyle sweater, and his gut filled the space between his chair and the table. He was busy deshelling and swallowing an entire bowl of peanuts. I bought him a pricey scotch and went to work.

I learned that he was married (thirty-six years and running), had four daughters (two in high school, two in college), was educated at a place named Bryant's Medical School (loser), was an absolute ping-pong addict, hated golf, and was missing the big toe on his left foot. Three hours into the conversation, when we were both pretty wet around the gills, I broached the subject. We'd mentioned Grandma only in a cursory fashion at the beginning of the evening. I'd carefully steered the conversation to other topics, but it was time to begin.

"I have a proposition for you," I said. I leaned forward dramatically so his mind would infer any number of lurid possibilities.

He started laughing and couldn't stop for an entire minute. He wiped tears from his eyes and managed to croak, "I'm married, son." It was obvious he didn't get out much.

It was a perfect reaction, lowered his guard just a little bit more. Then I cold-cocked him. I said I wanted to make a wager that he couldn't save my grandma.

When he realized that I was serious, he stood from the table. I'm surprised he didn't toss his drink in my face. He was that angry. His face deepened in its redness until I began to wonder if his airway was blocked. He was confused, drunk, pissed off, insulted, but he lingered at the table long enough to know that he was purposefully, though probably unconsciously, forfeiting his one chance to storm out of the bar. He was slightly – very, very slightly – curious. My proposal was an affront to his vocation, his dignity, his morals. His jowls shook at the hands of their neurological master, but he was attempting to suppress his instincts. He wanted to hear more. It took ten minutes of persuasion, and eventually he stayed to "hear me out."

That's why I had to bet on Death. I had dragged Socrates' pride to the railroad tracks and tied it down with heavy rope. The train was wailing in the distance, on its way toward him. His skills would be put to the ultimate test. To save a life is miraculous, but to save a life under threat of personal emasculation. . . .

It's what everyone wonders: if I had to perform this piano piece perfectly, from beginning to end, just one time, could I do it? If I was given one chance to toss this crumpled paper into the trash can from across the room or suffer eternal damnation in Hell, would I succeed?

I bought him another scotch, touching his elbow as I set the glass in front of him. As soon as I sat down, I began chiseling subtly away at him, but never cruelly, never taunting him.

"I guess it would amp up the pressure pretty high," I said.

He chuckled, a rumbling spasm that rocked the table. "You think life and death aren't high enough stakes?" He brushed peanut dust from his chest. He'd stopped making eye contact long ago, but he was still responding to my prompts. "You don't know a thing about pressure."

I let it rest for half a minute, as if considering what he'd said. Then I added, "But the money makes it too personal. I understand."

"It makes it unethical. Let's call a spade a spade."

"I've been tipping the server. To insure proper service. Is that unethical?"

And so on. I worked on him for the better part of two hours. The drinks kept coming. I played it without emotion. Doctors are reasonable people who respond to reasonable arguments. I described my family situation, all the deaths that had made up my life. I told him that I wanted to give Grandma a proper, respectful funeral and that she didn't have a life insurance policy. These things were true. In fact, I never lie to people. It's one of my most admirable qualities.

☆

The surgery took place at 1:00 PM. I walked alongside Grandma's gurney as they wheeled her down the corridor. She was too weak to hold my hand, too weak to raise her head or to move any part of her body, but her eyes had a lucid, greedy quality about them, as if she were absorbing everything, like a corpse given five more minutes to get one last look at things. I reflected on my family's strangely fragile genetic make-up. We were all damaged people, damaged by life.

Doctor Socrates was supremely detached and clinical in his brief pre-surgery discussion with me in the hallway while Grandma was being anesthetized. His assistant gave me papers to sign as the doctor explained the procedure once again, glancing over the tops of his bifocals at his ever-present clipboard. I searched his gestures, expressions, and vocal inflections for signals – I wanted to be sure the bet was still on, as I've been burned before by people who, after losing, claim not to have been serious in the first place.

A barely perceptible gesture before he walked into the operating room was enough to know. There was a shift in the way his eyes met mine. It was a flash of aggression, a flicker of a challenge. He was communicating something. Something like, "Just wait and see, you son of a bitch. You better have your checkbook ready." I wondered as he disappeared behind the door if he'd brought along cash or if his confidence was too high to allow that.

☆

Nothing remarkable had sprung from our family line. We were working-class types – mechanics, drywallers, movers, postmen – who'd carved a comfortable niche in the social space between the farm where my father grew up and the university that one in three of the Lawrence siblings had attended. My dad was a plumber for twenty-eight years, my mother a bank teller until she ran away with Wayne, at which point she didn't have to do any work because he was an engineer with an actual degree from college.

We Lawrences were all tired people. Even at a young age I was calm and placid to the point of being perceived as medicated. My parents were the same. The house was silent at most hours of the day and night. My father smoked cherry cigarillos and read catalogues in his armchair. My mom stitched up sweaters with the old, humming Singer. All of their hobbies involved total silence. Nobody shouted in our house. Nobody confronted problems. We kept everything inside. They were in bed and snoring by nine o'clock.

My alcohol use has been a real blessing. It serves to ignite me, to involve me actively with the world, to take those pond ripples I mentioned earlier and turn them into "hang ten"-type waves I can surf on. However, it's difficult to shake the sensation that all I'm doing is acting when I'm around other people, that my true self is inside me, playing solitaire with a double deck of cards on the coffee table, a dim lamp glowing in the corner of the room.

It's appropriate, I think, that so many deaths have occurred in my family over a short period of time. An underlying Lawrence sentiment has always been that the deceased is sort of lucky to be relieved of the burden of consciousness. From past funerals I remember comments like, "Well, now he doesn't have to work another day," or "He looks more peaceful than he ever did before," or, what Grandma said to me at my dad's wake, "He's living in his dreams now, Jerry."

Two weeks after Grandma's funeral, I received a brief letter from my mom, expressing her condolences. She enclosed a check for $200 with the sympathy card. The postmark was from Lincoln, Nebraska, which meant she had moved again and probably had a new boyfriend.

At the funeral, I met a few distant cousins for the first time. I shook their hands and talked to them about the weather. My great-aunt Thelma, ninety years of age, arrived in her wheelchair, which she'd decorated with black bows. I hadn't seen her since I was ten. Mostly, though, it was friends and acquaintances that Grandma had made over the years. Fifteen people stood at her graveside and watched her go into the ground. Keeping Grandma's "onion tear stimulation" theory in mind, I wore my sunglasses, but it didn't help.

Doctor Socrates made an unexpected appearance. During the final blessing of the body, I spotted him leaning against a tree a short distance away, watching. He wore a hat, something like a fedora, which concealed his face partially, and a gray trench coat. It struck me as a very cinematic moment. I touched the casket to say good-bye to my grandma and my friend.

I caught up with the doctor at his car. The first thing I did was pat him on the shoulder and say, "I didn't expect to see you here. Grandma would've appreciated it."

He brushed my hand away, grabbed his keys from his coat pocket, and told me in a whisper that I was a fucking bastard. His eyes were rimmed with red. He told me that if I ever tried to talk to him again he would personally break my legs. As a last gesture before driving away, he spat on the pavement near my shoes.

I miss Grandma. She never judged me, never criticized. I cried a few more times when I heard the theme song from *Murder She Wrote*. I kept all Grandma's photo albums, too, which make me choke up when I flip through them. Now that I have $2500 from the bet, along with the $3600 from Grandma's estate sale, I stay away from pool tables. My plan is to live off the money for four months, then hop a Greyhound and go find my mom.

I'm not going to yell at her. I'm not looking to squeeze an apology, or tears, out of her. I don't want to pick a fight with her or her new man. Sure, I plan on giving her Grandma's photo albums, and she's likely to see this as a provocation, filled as they are with pictures of my dad. And I'm certainly planning to hang around her as closely as I can, in her house if possible, in a nearby hotel if necessary, for a long, long time. Eventually, something's got to give. One of us will emerge as the clear victor.

I like to win bets. Anyone I know will tell you that I like to win. A pretty girl in a tank-top is nice, but betting is the more intense experience in the end. However, I'm not what many would call a typical gambler. Horseracing, NFL, NBA, NHL, the Major Leagues – those things don't interest me. If someone's going to break my legs I want it to be because I won, not because I lost.

The Big Baby Crime Spree

I. The Pretty New Nurse From Pediatrics

I'm standing behind my wife in the cafeteria line at St. Mary's. Except she's not my wife, not yet. Right now, she's just the P.N.N.F.P. On her tray she's got two Jell-O cubes in a bowl. I breathe deep and stutter twice before I'm able to spit out, "Is that all you're going to eat?!"

When she looks up, I want so bad to lick my hand, palm back this hair, and tell her that the Jell-O cubes match her green eyes. The skin on her cheeks is Wonder Bread, like it's never been hit by anything but air. Her only blemish is a tiny circular scar near the top of her forehead. She's got charcoal slashes for eyebrows, a hatchet nose, and no chin. She doesn't wear makeup or perfume, but still, she smells good. It makes me nervous to be this close to a musky-smelling woman, and then an actual thud – my heart – shakes my ribcage, and I realize that our meeting is the best coincidence!

We'll hit the highway doing ninety-five, the back of the Econoline screaming with the Crime Babies of the Crime Crib. I didn't know that I'd need, want, or meet a beautiful sidekick, but I'm rearranging the plan to fit her in. At the rest stops, we'll make love in the front captain's chair, then take turns pumping gas and bottle-feeding those money-grabbing babies, to make sure they aren't getting any ideas about crying too loud. I'll break out my roll of dimes and call Dad at The Home, where he'll have his own personal nurse (just like I will), his own private room with a couch, a TV, a bathroom – almost everything a real home has – so he'll never for one minute believe he's in a hospital.

My pretty nurse (her name tag: *Rhonda*) is wearing a cobweb smile. She's pondering something important – probably a guy she used to know, a guy who looks like me, a guy she loved, hated, or couldn't care less about. She keeps reading my feet, giving me nothing but that flimsy smile. She might want to stab my neck with a fork. She might want to plant a kiss on my lips. She might want to grab my hand and force me to point to the *exact spot* where my lazy left eye is focusing. (No one can tell which eye I'm looking with. FYI, it's both.)

I nod at her tray and say, "Not much for a growing woman."

She growls, "Some people don't *need* much."

She doesn't sound annoyed, just burned. She's a car engine that wants oil.

II. What Nobody Knows

I've handled so much poop in the last three years (on and off the job) that it's no more unpleasant than picking up a penny from the sidewalk. The bad stuff is the stuff that can't be picked up, and this is what Dad makes in the last couple months. Yesterday, though, from the supply closet I stole a box of jumbo panty liner pads meant to catch uterus blood after a baby comes out, so now I slide these into Dad's briefs, which I hope might help with laundry expenses.

Dad doesn't recognize a toothbrush, and he can't dress himself. He also can't dress a toothbrush and doesn't recognize himself. Quick flashes maybe once or twice a week are the exception, and during these he barks, "I'm not a goddamn baby, Travis!" in a tone that understands everything and tells me that I'm embarrassing him by stripping off his jeans for a bath. These flashes hurt the most. Real Dad appears, and I see a message in his eyes – that he appreciates what I've been doing, that he wishes it could be different, but that some things are inevitable. I see this in a five-second span. Then Real Dad vanishes and I wonder if it was all in my head, because he turns and begs the towel rack to let him pitch the last two innings (he played baseball in high school).

I don't know how old Dad is, and there's no one around to tell me. In the '70s and '80s he was a Dodge truck. In the early '90s after I graduated high school, he started showing the first signs of the Alzheimer's (although he never got diagnosed), and now, ten years later, he's a stripped Nova. He weighs 122 pounds, down from 193. His legs are cornstalks. Without my shoulder, he can't get out of bed. If there was a God, like Mom believes, Dad wouldn't be living *anywhere* anymore, but at least Dad's in the best place, which is his own place, which is our two-bedroom apartment, mine and his.

He hates hospitals like I do and made me promise when I was only seven that I would kidnap him or euthanize him if he ever got hospitalized. I remember asking, "Even if you only get your tonsils taken out?" He nodded with a serious face, but there was a spark in his eye, and I understood that he was joking, but also that the joke wasn't really a joke.

When I was eight, Dad sliced up the bottom of his foot by stepping on a sharp bone while swimming in a channel. He sutured himself with fishing line. When I was nine, he caught pneumonia and spent twenty days at home, refusing to go to the doctor. A year later, a pipe exploded at the caulking-glue factory where he worked, and he got second-degree scalding on the backs of his thighs. For four weeks he was on his stomach, swearing so loud I thought he'd break the windows. He ignored my mom's "Stop being a jackass and go to the hospital" (by then her shit just bounced off of him), and once a day I scrubbed away the dead skin with a Brillo pad and told him I was proud, that I didn't care that he wasn't getting "workman's cop," and that he was the strongest man in the world.

Mom's been giving tours of volcanoes in Hawaii since I was eleven, which is when she left me and Dad. She only meant to leave Dad, but I told her lawyer and the judge (I couldn't make myself look at her face) that no matter what, I wouldn't live with her. I like to imagine Mom leading a gang of tourists around the rim of Mt. Kilauea. One hand holds her hair in place while the other points at the big hole behind her: "You don't want to put this lava in a lamp."

Mom hates me and Dad so much that the last time I talked to her, which was two days ago (and before that eighteen months ago, and before that three years), she said, "Your father deserves everything he's getting. Whoremongers and adulterers will be judged."

I wanted to whack the receiver on the table until it shattered so I could bake the shards into Betty Crocker cupcakes, mail them to her, and make her choke.

Instead I told her, "It's a shame you feel that way," and asked if she would send money for cigarettes and other necessities. She agreed to wire cash (after I promised that Dad wouldn't get a dime of it), made a big deal out of telling me how quickly she'd get to the Western Union ("How's $1,000? Is that enough? I'm putting on my sneakers this minute!"), and basically pretended she's got a reborn pocketbook to match her reborn Christian heart. Same old routine. She won't send anything but prayers.

When I unlock the bedroom door, Dad sits up with bugging eyes and tries to bash me with the bedside lamp. I take the lamp from his hands and set it on the floor. He's not strong. I settle him down, cover him with a blanket. I tell him stories of things we did together, like grilling brats and corn cobs in Riverside Park, having a good laugh after buying a "boner" for our fishing trip from the blushing old lady at Ace Hardware, blasting M-80s in front of our house on Gratiot, toasting frozen pizzas in the iron 1940s oven that I called *Jabba the Hot* when I was small.

Dad stares across the room at things I don't see. I wonder how long it'll be before he's so gone that he's not my dad anymore. If there's a line, he's standing on it.

Once he's asleep I go into the living room. I pull the top notebook from the pile under the coffee table.

I need five babies. They'll have to be the tiniest newborns – anywhere from brand new to two months – so I can train them and use them before their fingerprints form. Most people don't know that babies don't have fingerprints at birth. The nurses take an ink stamp of the foot print after the baby pops out, which can identify it to some degree. And they have a hospital band that gets fastened around the baby's wrist, which sets off an alarm, locks all the doors, and kills the elevators if the baby's taken out of the ward. They have lots of security in place for these little people, but when a baby touches something with its fingers, it's like nobody was ever there.

III. The Motherfucking Mountain

I'm in the cafeteria, waiting for Rhonda, the P.N.N.F.P. Only I'm supposed to call her "Thelma," because Thelma Pickles was John Lennon's first girlfriend. I need to drill this into my head. I am NOT going to mess this up. This is my future wife. I also need to ask her about the book she's writing, so I will NOT tell her

73

about the Big Baby Crime Spree during our first food-break date.

I've seen Rhonda around the hospital every day since we met last week. When she passes me in the hallway, she looks me up and down like I'm a racehorse. The problem is that I can't tell what category of racehorse I am – loser, winner, stud or glue – because her green eyes just cover me like a heavy blanket.

The real surprise came this morning. I was heading to the elevator to go to Examination Room 409 when she popped out of Ultrasound. She stared into my eyes and smiled. I almost fell into the bucket I was pushing. This smile wasn't flimsy like her first one. We waited for the elevator together. She dove right into her John Lennon book, and her name preference, and I told her I wanted to hear all about it but that I had to get to Midwifery for vomit mop-up. She's the same height as me (5' 5"), and her front teeth are bucked out in a sexy way. It had to be destiny, so I asked her on this lunch date.

Here she comes. I run a finger along the bottom of the mustache to clear the hairs.

"Should we get some food?" she asks, and I let out a cool, "Yes ma'am."

I load my tray with barbeque chips, a Frisbee-sized Granny Elma's chocolate chip cookie, and an Extra Large root beer. Rhonda is having a blueberry muffin and a cup of hot Lemon Zinger tea, which are on me. I carry both trays to our table.

"Tell me about your book, Thelma."

"I brought it," she says. She plops down her bloated purse, which might weigh forty pounds. She sucks five fingertips before reaching inside for her notebook.

She slides the notebook across the table. I open it. Even though my eyeballs point goofy, I can read without glasses. Dad once told me that my eyes are this way because I'm curious about everything and my body wants to see as much as possible, so it splits itself.

"I have a mountain of letters at home," Thelma says. "A motherfucking MOUNTAIN! I kid you not." Her hand's a hatchet, and she starts chopping the air with it, like she wants to lop off the peak of the mountain. With her teeth she rips a wedge from her muffin in a way that scares and excites me. "I left the grammar mistakes," she says. Crumbs rain onto the table. "Just so you don't think I'm a dummy."

I start reading her notebook. What I see is a bunch of very brief letters, written in Thelma's own handwriting:

Oct 9, 2002

    Ricky (trufan@yahoo.com)

    Comments: john, I can hardly express my inside emotions and my . . . PAIN I miss you. thanks for sharing your insperation, care and smiles. Your one in a million and a blesing to us all.

Oct 9, 2004

    Flesym Evol (iamhe@hotmail.com)

    Comments: JOOHHHHNNN!!! You are LOVVE!! happy birthday!! John you'll be inside me always! Happy Birthday!

Oct 9, 2005

    Jerry Dove (penbutt@erthlink.com)

    Comments: Dear John: I want to sing "Happy Birthday" to you. But don't you wonder what happy birthday means to a dead guy like you. Thats like singing to a side of beef. Wasting time All I really would like to remind you on your 62nd birthday, is "Instent Karma". Without those words where would we be. To me you were somthing awsome. You were there for me when other's weren't. Like sadie you were beutiful John, and you will stay beutiful in my mind. You are more then a side of beef. You will live on . . . forever.

Thelma talks while I'm reading. She worshipped John Lennon and the Beatles her entire life and was horrified to hear that "John was assassinated in cold blood." She owns every Beatle album, every "John" album, Beatle photographs, books – it's a blur of "John John John John John" for fifteen minutes. Then she talks about a few years ago when she got so depressed on December 8th that she swore she'd do something to honor the next *October 9th* because that was a more positive way to spend her energy. I can't help wonder why he was "assassinated" while if I got shot, I would just be plain shot.

The story of Thelma's notebook (which she "will publish very soon") is that she posted a request on the Internet for birthday messages to John, but the tricky part is that she asked for only snail mail, because that's all they had in "John's era." She gave out her home address, and people have been sending letters ever since. When she receives the letters, though, she rewrites them in her notebook, in pen, in "email form" (whatever that means), so that they "seem more modern for the modern reader." It's all very confusing. I'm embarrassed that I don't know John Lennon, or the girl that Rhonda named herself after. I mean, I know the Beatles. I know who the guy is, but I can't picture him when she's telling me this stuff. He's one of the moppy British guys. The smart one, I think.

"These are written by *real people*, who have true, strong feelings for this man." Her bottom lip is a live wire. "These are *real letters*, Gary."

I'm used to being called "Gary," but it sounds weird coming out of Thelma's mouth, like she's not talking to me. Like I'm Gary, but Gary isn't me.

Nobody at the hospital knows that my name is Travis. On my job application three years ago I used my middle name because the Big Baby Crime Spree was already taking shape in my mind. I'd been a custodian at the Chic University of Cosmetology, and Dad was getting worse, and one day I saw a cosmetology student showing off pictures of her baby to her friends. I stood outside the classroom and listened, and that's when I learned about the Three-Month No Fingerprint Window. I went to St. Mary's the next day and applied.

Thelma reaches across the table to tap the notebook: "Read this one."

Oct 9, 2005
Pamela Pretty (neverded@erthlink.net)
Comments: This minnit I am liteing four canldes on October 9th. It is 1:27am and one each burns for John and Yoko, Julian and Sean. I am listening to Mind Games. I love you beutiful man. I am soooo lucky to have a good notebook like the one here to share my feeling about what you let us. You were an amazing man to me and my growing old. I will meet you somday.

"Why is she burning four candles?" I ask. "Are those other people dead?"

She looks at me like there's a beard on my teeth. "YOKO ONO? His WIFE?"

"What – "

"And his two SONS?"

"I guess she burns candles whether people are dead or alive."

Out comes a snippy, "Is there a difference?" She snatches her notebook, shoves it into her purse, and stares across the room.

"It'll be a great book," I say.

IV. She Invokes Jesus Because of the Black Cloud

She's been a nurse for ten years. She's older than me; she's thirty-seven.

She's never been married or had a kid, and she says the first part of this is true only because she's "ineligible" for the second.

The dime-sized scar on her forehead is from a dime that some "fuckface" dropped from the top of an office building when she was visiting Chicago with her parents during the seventh grade. She blames her infertility on this freak accident. She says the dime destroyed the part of her brain that tells her body NOT to treat an embryo like a foreign invader. She's had "at least six" miscarriages. It sounds crazy, but I believe her. There's a big connection between the brain and the body. I heard that juggling can ward off Alzheimer's, which is why I taught myself with apples.

Her parents don't like her. They got divorced when she was a senior, and both parents ended up in a Portland. Her dad's in Maine and her mom's in Oregon. Thelma's in Michigan, equally far from one as the other. I tell her my parents are divorced too, that my mom left after my dad had an affair with a lady who worked at the ice cream shop. I say I didn't blame Dad because Mom was always saying that his model airplanes were a waste of time, that his feet stunk, that his fingers had caulk on them, that he needed to wash his face before he could kiss her, and after the divorce Mom became a reborn –

"Finished?" Thelma says. "I'm pretty sure I was speaking."

Thelma enjoys kids, especially babies. She wants to be a midwife, but her supervisor told her she's too emotional.

She took me to her apartment after our lunch date, and she "really really really" wanted to show me the mountain of letters from Lennon fans, but the mountain was in a basement storage closet "so it would be a hassle." I sat on her couch and flipped through her notebook. I pretended to be fascinated while she made grilled cheeses. The notebook was interesting at first but so repetitive that it turned boring pretty fast. Every letter was about the same guy. A dead guy nobody would remember in a while except the people who loved him, and those people would probably be dead in a while too.

Also, the writing was mush. All sweet and overblown. I hate mush. Mush is what comes out of my dad.

Last, I didn't understand the purpose. It was like writing a book about the tree behind your house. The letters didn't accomplish anything. The tree didn't know or care about this jibber-jabber.

I kept wondering if we were going to do anything physical because Thelma popped out of the kitchen every two minutes when she was supposed to be slicing cheese, or bread, and practically sat on top of me to explain every single letter. I thought about kissing her, but there was never a long enough pause. She really liked to talk. Things were flowing, I guess. Between wanting to make out, wanting to share my plan, and wanting her to shut up, I couldn't tell what I wanted most.

I went to the kitchen sink to dump out our empty beer cans. That's when she stepped up and punched my lips with a kiss. Our teeth clacked. I tasted blood. We went to the couch and mashed until the sandwiches on the stove set off the fire alarm. The kitchen filled with smoke. We threw open the windows. Rhonda gasped for air. She stuck her head out the window and yelled, "Jesus please help us, we're gonna die in a black cloud," which froze me in my tracks.

Then she grabbed her Lennon notebook while I ran to tell the first-floor neighbors that it was nothing to worry about. An old woman answered the door. I could see the husband in the background peeking at me from a dark hallway. The woman yawned while I was telling her. When I assured her that the basement storage closets wouldn't be damaged, she fanned the air with her hand like she was shooing a fly. She shut the door in my face.

Rhonda came downstairs and asked if we could "finish hanging out" at my place. I didn't want to say yes, but I also didn't want to say no. So we went.

V. Record Albums Don't Break Easily

She doesn't want to kiss anymore. I take my hand off her boob. I can't look her in the eye.

"When you try *not* to," she says, "you end up staring straight at me."

"What did I do?"

"Not you, stupid. Your dad. What's he doing in there? It's extremely distracting."

"He gets confused, so he cries."

"And pounds the wall? And tells the lawyer from Saginaw to fuck a pile of pudding?"

"I'll put on some music." I go to the stereo.

"It's because you lock him in his room like an animal," she says.

What the hell does she know about it? But at least she's sitting down again. I keep one eye on her and one on the records. She's digging a pen out of her purse. The best album I can find is Stevie Wonder's *Songs in the Key of Life*. Dad's not crying anymore, but even worse, he's starting The Moan.

It's quiet for now. I don't think Thelma can hear it, but it'll get louder. I'm sliding the record out of the jacket as fast as I can.

Thelma's reading one of her letters aloud: "'You jealous child of nature! I do adore you for your poetry, your insecurity, your mistakes, your anger, your Lennon. Please be with me tomorrow, be always with me.' Did you hear that, Gary? *Be always with me.* This theme runs through every letter. John was imperfect, but his imperfections make him so incredibly eternal."

Dad's moan is sputtering, uuhuh . . . uhhuh . . . uuhhhhh; almost like a laugh; Thelma's forehead scar is turning whiter; my hands are shaking all over the place; got the turntable lid up, power on; uuhhhhhhhhhhhhhhhh.

"I'm thinking about taking little sections – just a line or a phrase – like the essence of certain letters, and suturing them together to make my own songs."

uuuUuuuuhHHHHh

"Do you think I'm talented enough to write my own songs?"; "Of course you're talented enough."; UUUuUuuuuUuuUU; "YOU WHAT?"; UuuUUUUUUUUUuUuuUUuuHHH hhhHhH-HHHHhhhhHHHHHH; stupid hands won't stop TREMBLING; "I'll bet you could write some FANTASTIC SONGS, Thelma"; UUUUHU "You're just saying that, aren't you?"UHHUHH-HHH"No way! I youUHUUhave HHHHUUNHtalent IHUH-HUHUHNNNNNYFFFNNNNNNNNNNUUUUHHHH "FOR CHRIST'S SAKE!" Thelma frisbees her notebook across the room. It knocks an ashtray off the end table. Cigarette butts explode in a cloud. She runs to the bedroom door, starts beating it with her fists. "CAN YOU SHUT THE HELL UP?!"

I run to her and start whacking her back with the Stevie Wonder record, but it just wobbles and warbles zzzzand slaps without even bothering him. She kicks the door, twists the knob; it seems like she really *would* run in there and smother him with the pillow if she had the chance. I have no choice but to tackle her. We end up on the bathroom floor. She bucks and screams and tries to knee my nuts. I start kissing her neck, and we end up making love on the cold tile with Dad groaning right along with us.

Later, I tell her my plan. We're still lying on the bathroom floor. Dad stopped moaning not long after we did. My head's resting on Thelma's shoulder. I haven't made love in six years, so my privates feel like a beach after a good rain.

"Who has B.O.?" she asks. She sniffs my armpit. "God, it's you."

I smell her armpit. "You, too."

"I hate being a nurse."

"I hate being a janitor."

"That's not what you said before."

"I don't hate it. It's going to make me rich. But not by cleaning toilets."

"My supervisor is a 100% nutcase. She wears plaid socks. *That's* creativity, to her. *That's* how she shows her individuality. What a waste." She starts singing, "*You think you're so clever and classless and free/But you're still fucking peasants as far as I can see.*"

"One of Lennon's masterpieces," I say. I've never heard it before, but obviously it's one of his songs. It sounds nice pouring out of the smoky hole of her mouth.

"I only got into nursing because my mom begged me. She wanted me to help people because she felt bad for hurting so many." She lets out a sharp laugh, then lights another cigarette as I drop her first one into the toilet. I'm enjoying her body odor and the proximity to her tits. She keeps talking. "I wanted to be a folk artist. I'm *great* with fabrics – I can make a whole outfit out of four square feet of burlap, including socks, and it's not nearly as uncomfortable as you might think, because I tenderize it with a warm dough roller – and actually, you'd be surprised how *nice* burlap can look. It makes people look more muscular than they are, which is something *everyone* can use now and then. You know, you would look *really* good in one of my outfits – *The Spy Who Loved Me* dinner vest would look incredible on you."

She shifts gears. "But who cares what I never did? I love the kids, hate the parents. I hate all parents. Parents can – " she clucks her tongue and flips the bird at the bathroom ceiling, " – sit and spin for all I care."

She thinks about it. She flicks something invisible off her right boob and says, "It's hard to hate someone who's dead, so I don't hate your dad. But I DO hate your mom, after what you told me."

It feels like the right time. I make my move. "We could help my dad."

"I'm listening."

"I have notebooks," I say. "Just like you."

VI. It's Like God Made Them Without Fingerprints Just for That Reason

She didn't laugh, and she didn't report me to the police. She sat hunched over my notebook for more than twenty minutes with a serious look on her face. Tears dropped out of her eyes. She thought the whole thing was beautiful.

"It's like God made them without fingerprints just for that reason." She dove on me; we made love for the second time. She made me promise to return the babies after we finished, so I placed my hand over my heart and swore on my father's future grave, which I realized I might be able to mark with an actual headstone, that the babies were nothing more than a loan.

Five babies had been worked out as Lowest Risk with Highest Payoff Potential, which I calculated using a formula that took two weeks to create. "Two weeks on just the *formula* to *calculate* the *calculation*!" I emphasized. Then I explained how it had taken three months of considering each possible heist scenario – convenience stores, bowling alleys, banks with armed guards, rich old ladies walking through East Town – with each possible number – two babies, three babies, four babies, five babies – before I'd come to my final decision. "I will not rush this plan," I told her. I explained that for three years I had ignored even the urgent nature of Daddy's illness and my desperate need to reach a different station in life, and that I had proceeded slowly and carefully, like a tortoise climbing a mountain.

She said she loved my plan and gave me a number of what she called "extreme hugs."

At work the next morning, though, I turned nervous. I couldn't keep my hands from trembling when I peeked through the NICU window. She'd accepted The Big Baby Crime Spree so quickly, without question. She even went into Dad's room for a while, with the door closed. I could hear her talking softly. The words were impossible to understand. She had sworn not to tell him about my plan.

It felt suspicious. Still, this was the reaction I'd wanted, so why was I upset? She hadn't made me feel like a hopeless asshole, which I had expected.

I kept with the plan. For the next few days I hung around Midwifery more often than normal, because my calculations had determined that they were a safer bet than Obstetrics. The pregnant women under Midwives' care were mostly teenaged, unwed moms whose babies would be candidates for NICU, moms with low incomes who might not even be eager to bring their babies home. By eavesdropping I'd learned that most NICU babies were basically healthy, that they had minor problems like jaundice, slightly swollen kidneys, fluid in the lungs – nothing fatal – and they were kept there as a precaution so the hospital wouldn't get sued if they died.

I entered the Midwifery receptionist's office whenever it was unstaffed to "empty the trash" while I eyeballed the patient files. A boom month was right around the corner; seven teen moms were due during a two-week period, and we had a regular stock of at least five infants in ICU (all less than one month old).

I ran over the possibilities. Twelve or more babies to choose from. I was sure to get the five we needed. All the money they would grab in those tiny hands. All the incredible van sex. I would move Dad into a Home where a kind nurse would sit by his bed twenty-four hours a day. I would tell Mom where she could stick her nonexistent money and her nonexistent God.

Beyond these details I couldn't see much else.

After work on Friday I told Thelma about the upcoming baby boom.

"It's a sign from heaven," she told me.

This was the last straw. I couldn't hold my tongue. I hadn't said anything about the "God made them without fingerprints" comment, or the "Jesus please help us," so this time I exploded. I told her I didn't believe in heaven and that I was horrified to have a Christian as a crime partner. We argued in the hospital parking lot. She threw an egg roll at my head. I told her that John Lennon didn't believe in heaven – I knew *that* much about the guy.

She said, "If you're talking about 'Imagine,' I don't need to tell you that he was saying that no heaven was a terrible thing to think about. 'Above us only sky?!' 'It's easy if you try?!' The easy way out is to not believe in anything! It's seductive and blue! He saw his own death years before it happened! He saw it in a bowl of miso soup the night he dropped nine hits of acid and got Yoko pregnant with *triplets* that she miscarried *three months to the day* into her pregnancy! Think about *three* for a minute. Surprise! Ever hear of The Holy Trinity? Don't talk to *me* about John Lennon! 'Only SKY?' *Death*! He didn't want to be without heaven! Nobody does! And that doesn't mean I'm a Christian!"

I didn't back down and neither did she. We yelled until the parking attendant threatened to call the police, then we drove to West Main Cemetery in our separate vehicles.

By the time we arrived, the anger had worn off. It felt good to have let off some steam. It'd been months since I'd talked to anybody except my mother, the other janitors, and the guys at the Dairy Mart. Thelma never talked to anyone besides the other nurses. This was our first great moment, in the back of my Econoline, after the fight about God's existence, turning our anger into sex.

After sex, though, Thelma restarted her argument. She smoked half a pack of cigarettes before I could get a word in. By the time she ran out of steam, I had lost all desire to fight. And so, in a way, I conceded that heaven existed. It was belief by surrender.

VII. Once in a While It Sounds Like

Thelma says babies are like pets. You program them with words they can't understand, and they can't disobey until they're able to understand the real meanings, which is at least one year. She quotes Doctor Spock, Doctor Phil, and her nurse friend, Pammy.

According to Thelma, her own shithead parents succeeded in raising a charmed daughter who's never gotten caught shop-lifting in 217 attempts, so she knows a thing or two about the psychology of stealing.

No matter where we are – her apartment or mine – she pesters me about the Wheres, Whats, Whens, Whos, and Hows. She asks questions like, "What entrance should we park near?" "What will we say when someone sees us with the duffel bag full of babies?" "How can we keep the babies quiet but full of oxygen for the time required to escape the hospital?" "How do you know that the coating of KY Jelly will really stop the ankle bands from triggering the alarm?"

"How about reading this?" I flip the pages of my 3-Subject notebook in front of her nose. "I don't have the time to explain it all. Just trust me and do what I say."

I go back to my apartment, to the hand-drawn graph taped to the refrigerator. I've been crossing off the Estimated Days until the Big Baby Crime Spree (ten and counting) between feeding Dad his baby food and washing his legs after he messes himself.

Dad stays alive. In bed he curses, kicks, pees, mumbles, and rolls. His face is the color of the bathtub. When I come into the room he commands me to "Come clean, come clean." I don't know where he picked up this line, and I try not to care. He weeps until his pillowcase is soaked and then wobbles to the window to look at the clouds. His craziness is cute; it has to be cute. Otherwise it's punishment, and Mom was right all along. Maybe he knows about my plan. What else could he mean when he says, "Come clean?"

He keeps saying it as the days pass. Once in a while it sounds like *kill me*. His chest rattles. It sounds like his ribs are crumbling. Thelma comes over more often. She spends long stretches at his bedside, singing to him. I stand in the doorway and realize that's what Mom did with me when I was a boy.

VIII. I Asked Dad: Do You Think You'll Go to Heaven When You Die?

He said, "That snake just jumped the train to Battle Creek. Eight of us. Guys and girls getting shit-faced. Don't get a haircut tonight, no way."

Things are tense between me and Thelma. She believes in heaven. She turns the pages of my notebook, making faces, shouting "Oh, come *on*!" She composes lists of items that "we really need to buy for your 'Crime Spree'" (she even shows sarcastic finger quotation marks), and when I refuse to read her lists, she crumples them loudly and says, "I *thought* you might say that."

She comes over every day after work, and today, the day before the Crime Spree, is no different. We stand in the parking lot of my apartment. In her nurse outfit she looks so beautiful that I want to injure myself. I cough a few times.

"I think I have a fever."

"You don't say."

She's next to my Econoline with her arms crossed while I tell her that I've been doing some serious thinking. My initial calculations, I say, were made for me, for one person, and now that she's going to be my accomplice I'll need to make some major adjustments before we can safely move ahead. She pulls a notepad and pen out of her fat purse. She jots stuff while I say that it shouldn't take long – weeks, definitely; a few months, possibly – before we can start waiting for another baby boom, and then we'll be good to go.

She tears off a sheet of paper and hands me a note: *You will see now what some one can do with out interupsion or carful planing. Do not follow.*

She walks to the door and lets herself in with the key that I stupidly had copied for her.

I see her notebook on the back seat of her Bug. I open her car door with the key she stupidly had copied for me. I throw her terrible maroon 5-Subject notebook onto the pavement. I get on all fours and read the bullshit emails written in her own hand. All written for dead John Lennon with phony author names followed by phony words from phony minds that are all Thelma/Rhonda. Every letter sounds the same because every letter is the same, because there isn't any mountain except in her head, and there isn't a *real* letter within three thousand feet of Thelma, and Thelma is NOT her name. How could she think I was that stupid? She was going to publish these in a book? Laughable. Her plan was impossible before she even hatched it. She filled a notebook with denial.

I kick her notebook around the parking lot for ten minutes. I want to shred every page, fill the sky with her wasted ideas, but I don't. I tuck the book under my arm and storm inside, yelling that she's a fake and that I can prove it.

Rhonda's in my living room, kneeling over Dad's body.

IX. What Makes the Answer Correct

I run to him. He's a folded mannequin on the floor: stiff, half-naked, facedown. His eyes are wide as if shocked to see the carpet two inches from his face. His neck is red. He's wearing blue boxers and a white T-shirt. When I touch his arm the skin isn't cold, but it's less than warm. At this point, he's crossed the line. He's not my dad anymore. Why does he look so much like him?

Rhonda says something: "He can't be trained now," or something like that. My fingers touch him here and there – shoulder, forehead, elbow – because I expect to find the button that'll start him back up. I talk into his ear thinking maybe his brain is like a record player being turned off in a gradual way, noises slowing, warbling, winding down. I cradle his head. I pretend that this is one of those moments when he's himself. I tell him how the babies will be doing us a great service without even knowing it, how their ignorance means they have no guilt or regret or any of those moods that make the day so terrible.

Rhonda grabs me by the shoulders. She slaps my face. "Your name is *Travis*, you liar! And your dad did *not* deserve what he lived through!"

"Your name is *Rhonda*, and you never got a single letter from a John Lennon fan, and you don't know how to spell."

"John Lennon said that death is getting out of one car and getting into another, so at least your dad's got a destination. *Your* plan? Babies can't be trained. They can't control their *limbs*.

And the baby's fingerprints come in at three months – oh yeah, you got that right – when the *fetus* is three months old! Your idea was screwed from the beginning, and I just thought it was hilarious that you were so serious about it."

"You're wrong."

"I read your other notebooks, too. How's that Big Wig Black Market Blitz coming along? How many wigs did you actually make from the floor sweepings at the Cosmetology School? Or better yet, how's the Great Dunkin' Donut Apron Scam?"

I don't have anything to say.

"That thing on the floor. *That's* your Big Baby. Your father is way beyond that pile of skin."

I stare at the cracks in the ceiling plaster, cracks like a cobweb.

"I swear he was smiling when I did it," I hear Rhonda saying. "Don't make that face. Don't hate the messenger. Don't hate nature. Your dad stepped out with dignity. . . ." And then it's only her mouth making meaningless sounds. Suddenly, I understand why Dad lost his ability to talk to other people.

I roll over on the carpet. Dad's behind me somewhere.

My wife, my nurse, is killing the silence, filling it. I hope she keeps talking (she will). I hope she crawls to me (she will). I hope she leans over me (she will).

I hope she sings me a song, sings me my dreams.

Notes

Notes

Notes

Notes

Notes